PLAIN OBSESSION

ALISON STONE

TREEHAVEN PRESS

This book is a work of fiction. The names, characters, places, and incidents
are products of the writer's imagination or have been used fictitiously and
are not to be construed as real. Any resemblance to persons, living or dead,
actual events, locale or organizations is entirely coincidental.

PLAIN OBSESSION
Treehaven Press
Copyright © 2017 by Alison Stone

Editor: Julia Ganis, JuliaEdits.com.
Cover Art: The Killion Group

Be the first to learn about new books, giveaways, and deals in Alison's
newsletter by signing up online at AlisonStone.com

To my husband and kids, love you guys always and forever

CHAPTER 1

iolet flicked off the cap of the medicine bottle and shook out one tiny pill. She studied it in the palm of her hand and popped it into her mouth.

It seemed like such a Jacque thing to do.

People *had* always told her that she had reminded them of her mother and this was the first time in her twenty-seven years that she suspected they might be right.

Violet Jackson had resisted the siren call of the small bottle for the entire drive over here, but now she feared she'd pass out or her heart was going to beat out of her chest. Someone would find her unconscious in her little red sports car parked alongside the country road and the rumors would start anew.

You can do this.

Deep breath. In through her nose. Out through her mouth.

Violet stared up at the neat farmhouse where her dear friend Abby had once lived. The young Amish girl had come a long way from this farm in Hunters Ridge to becoming an assistant in Jacque Caldwell's business empire.

All because of her friendship with Violet.

All because of her…

She pinched the bridge of her nose, trying to hold back the wave of grief that had swelled and was ready to swamp her at a moment's notice. Drowning her.

Deep breath. In through her nose. Out through her mouth.

The calming effects of the medication began to take the edge off. She had white-knuckled it all the way here, even though she hated driving, and yet she couldn't continue to push through her rioting emotions to face what came next.

Rolling her shoulders, she knew she couldn't sit here forever. Her red sports car wasn't exactly incognito among the Amish farms and buggies that made up most of the population of Hunters Ridge, New York, a sleepy town in Western New York.

Touching the bottle through the fabric of her coat pocket like a talisman, she reached for the car door handle with the other.

"Okay…" she breathed out loud to herself. "You can do this." *You have to do this.*

By the time Violet reached the hard earth of the farm's driveway, she was amazed that all her panic symptoms had broken up and drifted away like the white floaties in the air after a wish on a dandelion.

The cornfields had been harvested for feed by equipment and horses from a long-ago era. She had watched the process from a distance when she'd lived in Hunters Ridge as a teenager. Only a small section of the field remained. They'd have to hurry. Silver clouds hunkered down on the horizon threatening snow. The beginning of November was a bit early for the white stuff, even for this part of the country. That's why she had to reach out to Abby's family today. Because once it snowed, she'd never find the nerve to drive.

By the time she reached the front porch, her sweaty hands and heart palpations were gone. It was a strange feeling, like she had kicked back a glass or two of wine. Courage without having to work for it.

Violet didn't know if Mrs. Graber was home, but she suspected she'd be in the kitchen preparing a meal for her husband and three children.

She used to have four.

Violet's shoes clacked on the bare wood of the porch, echoing in the stillness of the afternoon. The farmhouse looked neat and simple. Abby, two years younger than Violet, had marveled at all the fancy things found at the big house on the hill, as all the locals called Jacque Caldwell's country estate. Violet wondered not for the first time how differently things would have been if Abby hadn't come to work for her mother when she had finished up her eighth grade education, all that was allowed.

Sadness, Violet's constant companion, struggled to get its vicious claws into her. Thanks to the meds pumping through her veins, it was loosening its hold even as she wondered what she was doing here. What did she truly expect?

Clearing her throat, she lifted her hand to knock and the door flew open as if someone had been standing inside waiting for her. That, however, was doubtful. If they had, they probably would have stopped her at the end of the driveway. Chased her back to her car. Tried to keep the outsider out.

Staring back at her was Elmer Graber, Abby's brother. He had been only fifteen when he hitched up the horse and buggy and met his sister at the fast-food restaurant in town. He had brought along his younger twin sisters to say goodbye to their big sister Abby who was leaving Hunters Ridge and the Amish way for good.

Gone was the chubby-faced teen. The sadness in his eyes had been replaced by a steely gaze.

A half smile flickered across her lips at the sight of him, but if he recognized her, he didn't show it.

"Elmer, it's Violet."

"I know who you are." His harsh response might have had a more chilling effect on her thirty minutes ago.

"Is your mother home?"

"*Yah*, but that's no business of yours." He blocked the doorway, as if she might force her way inside.

"Please, I'd like to speak to her." She tapped her thumb from one finger to the next, a habit a long-ago therapist had taught her to distract herself.

"Who's there, Elmer?" A woman Violet had only seen at a distance approached, drying her hands on a dishtowel.

"Hello, Mrs. Graber, I'm Violet Jackson. Abby's friend." The words felt like a lie on her lips. *Some friend.*

"Abigail," Mrs. Graber said. "Her name was Abigail."

"Yes, of course."

All the color seemed to drain from the Amish woman's face. Elmer took his mother's arm and directed her to a wooden bench flanked by two rocking chairs in a sitting room off the entryway.

Violet stepped inside and paused, struggling to remember why she had come here in the first place. Was she being selfish? Looking to make herself feel better at the expense of the Graber family?

"I don't mean to upset you. I wanted to stop by and tell you how sorry I am about Abigail." Her dear friend had preferred her nickname.

Mrs. Graber sat silently, wringing the dishtowel, her bonneted head tipped forward.

"Is this why you have come? To upset my mother?" Elmer asked.

4

"No, absolutely not." Violet fingered the cuffs of her coat and wondered why she had thought this was a good idea. "Abby—Abigail—was my best friend and I feel awful about what happened."

Mrs. Graber lifted her head and stared at Violet with watery eyes. "My biggest regret in life is that I allowed my daughter to take that job working for your family. She was too young. Impressionable. It was the devil's work, making her want what she couldn't have."

The venom in her tone chipped away at the fuzziness dulling Violet's panic.

"Abigail enjoyed her life. She was happy." Violet wasn't sure this was what mattered to Mrs. Graber. Actually, she knew it wasn't. Abby had told Violet a lot about the Amish way of thinking during their long talks at the mansion. Two teenagers from very different worlds had bridged the gap. Violet had needed a friend. And Abby was looking for a way out.

Shoes sounded on the stairs. One of Abigail's twin sisters stood on the bottom step. The resemblance to her deceased sister was striking.

"Hi, Violet," she said shyly. She must have been listening from the top of the stairs.

"Stay in your room," Elmer yelled.

The teenager, Violet guessed seventeen or eighteen now, turned and bolted up the stairs without a complaint.

Elmer strode past Violet and opened the door wide. "You need to go."

Violet blinked slowly and nodded. "I'm sorry. I truly am." She turned to leave, realizing all the stories she had heard about the Amish and forgiveness didn't apply in this situation. Why should they? The Amish were human. The Graber family wasn't ready to forgive her.

Maybe with time.

But even time wouldn't bring Abigail back.

And no one could blame Violet more than she blamed herself.

A brisk wind whipping in from the west smacked her in the face as she jogged toward her car. She didn't dare turn around, but she could feel the eyes of hatred boring into the back of her head from somewhere on what once was a peaceful Amish farm.

$\mathcal{T}$heo Cooper hung up the phone after talking to one of his suppliers and leaned back. The torn leather on the arm of the office chair scraped against his forearm. The chair gave an ominous groan as he reached across and stretched the slats of the grimy blinds with two fingers.

His gaze traveled to the warehouse across the parking lot, then toward the road. No one. He released the blinds and reconsidered all the reasons why hiring Violet Jackson, even if only temporarily, was a bad idea. Sure, Cooper and Sons Lumber needed to get their books in order, and his dad knew a guy who'd suggested the perfect temporary hire.

But Violet…

Theo let out a long breath. He would have put the brakes on the suggestion if he had known who it was. By the time he found out, it would have been too rude to cancel the interview. Never in a million years would he have guessed Violet was back in Hunters Ridge. She had zipped out of here after high school graduation in a fancy limo, the same way she had arrived four years earlier.

Too good for this small town.

Too good for him.

He supposed he wasn't blameless in the way things had ended, but he was the kind of guy who didn't like to look back. Live and let live and all that. Regrets were for the weak. Something nudged at the base of his brain, suggesting he wasn't being exactly honest, but Theo didn't find much use in rehashing the past. He rubbed a hand across his mouth and wondered if his thoughts had always been this philosophical and cliché-ridden.

He leaned forward and the chair squeaked again. He scanned his humble office with a critical eye. *Humble* was being kind. This office was a step below humble. He and his cousin Chad, the co-owners of Cooper and Sons Lumber, had a thriving business, but were too busy running the day-to-day operations to make much-needed office improvements. He wondered if Hewlett and Packard had felt this way in their garage.

Ahhh. He smiled to himself. If only. Cooper and Sons was successful in that it provided jobs in the small community, but not big-time successful, which led him back to wondering why Violet would give them the time of day.

However, if he and Chad had any hopes of continuing to successfully run the business, they had to get the accounting books in order. Theo's father had maintained the books until his heart attack this past May, six months ago, which led to his forced early retirement in Florida. Since then, neither Chad nor Theo had prioritized bookkeeping. They kept up with bills and payroll, but that was it. They needed to get things in order.

Truth be told, prior to his dad's heart attack, Theo lived a thousand miles away, fully intending to make the army his career. But his priorities changed when his dad's health took a turn.

A solid knocking sounded on the door and snapped him out of his meandering thoughts.

Theo could have stretched from his chair and opened the door, but he thought better of it. He stood, plastered on a friendly smile and yanked open the door, and his greeting died on his lips. The nine years since high school had been kind to Violet. Pretty in high school had morphed into all-out stunning, even if she did try to play it down.

"Um..." Violet's dark eyes flashed, and a confused look swept across her face. "Hi, Theo... I have an interview with your dad?" Her statement came out more as a question. "Is he in?"

"No, he's not." Theo smiled at the young Amish woman who had shown Violet to his office. "Thanks, Lorianne. I'll take it from here."

Lorianne nodded her bonneted head, then hustled across the lot to the warehouse where a crew of mostly Amish workers cut and stacked wood for backyard play set kits.

Violet seemed to give the Amish woman a double take, then turned and smiled tightly at Theo, confusion in her big brown eyes.

"Please come in, it's freezing out there." He made an exaggerated show of looking up at the sky. "Looks like winter is coming early to Hunters Ridge."

"Yeah, winter's coming." Based on the quick wince, he could tell she regretted the trite weather comment. She turned to face him in the small space. The top of her head reached his chin, perfect for resting her head on his chest for a slow dance. He quickly shook the thought away.

"I trust you found the place okay?"

"Yes, but I was under the impression that I was meeting with your dad. I guess I'm a little confused."

"Perhaps that's my fault. My father set up the interview. He said he knew someone who knew someone." He made a rolling gesture with his hand. "You know how it is in a small town? He didn't tell me it was you until a few days ago."

"Isaac Weaver, the caretaker at my mother's property, told me your father was looking for some short-term help. I thought..." She let her words trail off, not finishing. Violet tugged on one end of her scarf and unthreaded it from around her neck. She slipped her arms out of her coat. She had always been trim, but she seemed even thinner now. Her cheeks were flushed, no doubt from the howling winds. "If this is too weird..."

"No, no..." Besides, where was he going to find another accountant on such short notice?

Violet glanced around the office, her long brown hair draping over her shoulders and down to her elbows. She wore it shorter in high school, but both styles were flattering. Violet never had to try at being pretty. It came naturally, even though she didn't seem to realize it. She had always been more focused on school, which apparently had served her well.

An awkward silence stretched between them and Theo suddenly realized he had been staring. He laughed, trying to hide his embarrassment, and held out his hand to an extra chair tucked between the desk and the couch. "Please, have a seat. Can I get you something? I used to have a coffee machine in the corner, but it conked out. There's fresh coffee in the warehouse across the parking lot."

"I'm fine." She smoothed a hand down her coat and sat. She struck him as very reserved, but then how would he know what she was like? He hadn't laid eyes on her in almost a decade.

Theo cleared his throat and decided to get right down to business. "We need an accountant to get our books in order. My dad kept the books until his sudden retirement last May." He rubbed the back of his neck. "This should be a short-term job. How long do you plan to be in town anyway?" He hoped he sounded as cool as he thought he did.

Violet's red lips curved into a tight smile. "For a little while." She crossed her legs and hugged the coat closer to her body. "I'm in a career transition." Her lips tightened into a straight line. "I understand you only need someone temporarily. It fits my timeline."

Theo studied the way she threaded and unthreaded her fingers while she talked. Had something happened that brought her back to Hunters Ridge?

"Yes, definitely temporary. Remember my cousin Chad? He's my business partner. We both think we can handle the record-keeping once we get organized."

"I've managed my mother's business for years and have gotten away from accounting, but before I went to work for Jacque I majored in accounting. I'd be happy to give you a hand."

"Can I ask why you're interested?" He could tell the question was too personal by the way the color drained from her face.

"Does it matter?" she asked flatly.

"I suppose not. Can you start tomorrow?"

"Sure." Violet glanced toward the door, then back at him. She struck him as distracted. "Tell me a little bit about the business."

"My grandfather started this company when my dad and uncle were boys. Basic lumberyard. My uncle died about ten years ago. A handful of years ago, my dad started a side business of making play sets. Some of them are pretty elaborate, almost like tree houses. I've even started designing some myself. My dad took care of the bookkeeping. After his illness, we got behind." He tapped a sketch in front of him for one of his more recent designs: two turrets, a tire swing and a climbing wall. "We've gained a reputation for quality and

11

we have to work all winter to fill orders for when the weather improves." Theo was determined to make sure his dad could continue to afford retirement in the Sunshine State for as long as he wanted. It was the least Theo could do for his dad after giving him such a rough time while he was growing up. He now understood how hard it was to be a single dad raising a son.

"The books haven't been maintained properly since your father left?"

Theo smiled sheepishly. "I'm afraid not. My dad kept a ledger." He pulled out a drawer to show her. "I started an excel spreadsheet, but mostly we got behind." He felt strangely self-conscious. Theo knew his strengths, but he generally didn't allow himself to feel embarrassment for his weaknesses. He was perfectly good at numbers, just not at organization. The former high school troublemaker turned army captain turned businessman felt inadequate sitting across the desk from someone who had far more education and business savvy than he would ever have.

Who cared if they had once sat next to each other in algebra class and had actually been friendly? Too much life had gotten between them. Money had provided her a wealth of opportunities. His working-class roots hadn't afforded him that same luxury

"It's not that I can't do the books," Theo added quickly. "I don't have time." He pulled open a side drawer and lifted up a wad of papers. "All these receipts have to be organized. I manage to pay the bills and payroll, but that's about it."

Violet tipped her head. "I can help you with that." She fidgeted with the button on the coat stretched across her lap.

"Are you okay?" Theo asked, studying the delicate features of her face.

"I'm fine." She jerked her head back and laughed, as if he

had asked a ridiculous question. "What time would you like me to come in tomorrow?"

"Does nine work?"

Violet nodded. "Will I be working in here?" She glanced around the small office trailer. A space heater in the corner spewed out warm air that smelled slightly of burnt dust with a hint of corn chips.

Theo couldn't help but smile. "Will that be a problem?"

She slowly shook her head. "I'll dress for the weather." A slow smile brightened her face.

Theo wanted to ask her how she'd been, but he figured they'd have plenty of time to catch up now that she was going to be working for him. He cleared his throat when the silence stretched too long.

"Definitely." He scooted out from behind the desk. "I'll show you out."

With a solid tug, Violet yanked the door open and a rush of cold air filled the small space. "No need, I found it." A hint of amusement lit her eyes. She paused in the doorway. "The Amish woman who showed me your office…"

"Yeah?"

"What's her name?"

"Lorianne. Lorianne Graber. Why?"

Violet's eyes widened and then she quickly schooled her expression. "She looked familiar, that's all."

Theo nodded, but sensed there was something more to it. "The employees here are predominately Amish. Hard workers."

"I'm sure they are."

Theo stood and watched the shadow of Violet through the thin shade as she pulled the door closed from the outside. Never in a million years did Theo think he'd have Violet Jackson working for him.

With a sense of satisfaction, he plopped down in his chair.

13

It squeaked as he tilted back. He traced the torn leather on the chair's arms and made a pledge right then and there not to get involved, despite all the old feelings suddenly coming to the surface.

Theo gathered up his sketches. He really should put them on the computer, but something about the hand-drawn sketches seemed quaint.

Tapping the edge of the papers on the desk, he thought about Violet's pretty smile.

Knock it off, buddy. You're not traveling down that road again.

~

Violet stepped onto the metal stoop of Theo's trailer-slash-office and was relieved when the frigid air cooled her fiery cheeks. She did it. She had left the safety of her house, sat through an interview and didn't make a fool of herself.

How far I've fallen from my world travels with my mother's business ventures.

She grabbed the railing and closed her eyes and reveled at how the meds contained the familiar tangle of raw nerves and anxiety.

She had indeed forced herself out of her comfort zone, but not without a little help. The reality dulled her victory. For weeks she had been holed up at the mansion, determined to win against her panic without medication.

She had done it as a teen. She could do it again.

Glancing over her shoulder at the closed trailer door, she hoped Theo didn't notice her fidgeting. He wasn't someone she trusted to be sympathetic.

Now how was she supposed to share this small space with him every day without white-knuckling it through her panic? She refused to rely on medication. Was she just being stubborn?

She tapped her fist on the cold railing, then made her way to her car, picking her steps carefully over the dusting of snow that had fallen during the short interview. The forecasters had predicted snow, but she never believed it till she saw it.

Tomorrow she'd dress more appropriately, too. No one here wore business attire. She should have thought of that. This was Hunters Ridge, not New York or Los Angeles.

Even the owner of the company wore jeans and a knit sweater that stretched across his broad chest, not that she should have been thinking of her new boss in those terms. She had been struck by how much Theo had filled out over the years. His face had transformed from boyish good-looking to ruggedly handsome. The shadow of a beard was a nice touch, too. Someone had probably already scooped him up, not that she cared.

The cool breeze at her open collar snapped her out of her musings. Ugh, she'd never get used to this. The dark clouds had moved in and big snowflakes fell on her eyelashes. How had she ended up here? Looking for a job as a bookkeeper in sleepy little Hunters Ridge?

She could hear Betty suggesting she dig deep. Find faith. Comments that always made her bristle. Hadn't Abby been faithful? Probably the most faithful person Violet had ever met. And now she was dead.

Figuring she should take advantage of the relaxed feeling she was riding, Violet glanced around, looking for Abby's little sister, Lorianne. The young Amish woman had escorted Violet to the office but hadn't seemed to recognize Violet from the fast-food restaurant five years ago when she bade her sister farewell.

Violet glanced around, but decided searching for Lorianne in the facility would have to wait for another day. Encouraged that she might be able to make amends—if only to find some peace herself—she aimed her key fob at the car door and the lights on her little sports car flashed.

"Not exactly a winter car."

Violet spun around, surprised to find Theo crossing the parking lot, his hands shoved in the pockets of his winter coat. Flakes of snow dotted his short dark hair. She forced a laugh, but feared it sounded uneasy. "I hadn't planned on spending the winter in Hunters Ridge when I bought it." She blinked away another snowflake from her lashes. "I rarely drove in the city. Period."

A smile seemed to come easy to his lips. It always had. He was an easygoing teenager who had cut class, got caught with beer at the football games, and seemed unfazed that he *was* the cool clique, picking and choosing who was in and who was out.

How could seeing someone from high school make me feel just like I was back there?

"Want a ride?"

Violet glanced at her car. A thin layer of light snow covered the windshield. "No, I'll be fine. I don't believe the forecasters called for much snow." She tucked a strand of hair behind her ear. "I suppose I should get used to it."

Theo flipped up his collar. "Are you sure I can't give you a ride? I have to drop some forms off in the warehouse, but after that I'm running an errand."

She flicked her wrist in dismissal, then opened her car door. The snow fluttered off the roof and landed on her seat. She bent over and swiped it away with her bare hand, aware Theo was watching her.

She straightened and said, "See you tomorrow."

"I'll let my cousin know you've accepted the job. I told him you were stopping by today. He bet you'd never show. He was wrong." He dragged a hand through his hair, the lines around his smiling eyes deepening, as if he'd perhaps realized he had said too much. "We both thought perhaps this job would be too boring for you."

"Not as boring as staring at the four walls of my mother's house." As soon as she said the words she immediately regretted it because the follow-up questions weren't ones she wanted to answer.

"I believe that house has far more than four walls." He squinted against the increasing snowfall. "Are you sure you don't want a ride home?"

"If I get going now, I'll make it home before it gets worse." She climbed into her car. "See you tomorrow at nine."

"Nine it is."

Inside her car under the thin layer of snow covering her windshield, Violet unbuttoned her coat and let out a long breath.

"I can do this," she muttered to herself. "You are not going to let panic control you." Absentmindedly she touched the hard bottle through the fabric of her coat pocket.

Shoving aside her spiraling thoughts—because they were certainly not helping her nerves, even with the meds—Violet turned on the wipers and the snow disappeared in a single swoosh. She turned on the front and rear defrosters, then powered down the side windows to clear the snow from them. Living in Hunters Ridge as a newly minted driver had taught her a thing or two—mainly how to effectively clear the snow from all windows without getting out of the car.

The rear defroster took a minute to clear the window. She tried not to think of the drive home, but she couldn't help it.

The thought of sending up a prayer crossed her mind, but she figured that would be too hypocritical considering how angry she was with God lately.

"Here goes nothing," she whispered. Glancing in the rear window with its perfectly delineated defroster lines, she put her little sports car into reverse and backed out of her spot. She had to rock backward before she could gain traction to pull onto the main country road. Despite everything, her palms were already sweat slicked. She tugged on her seatbelt and let out a long breath through tight lips.

Focus on the road, not on your shortness of breath, your heart rate, your dizziness...

Violet blinked rapidly. The snowflakes were mesmerizing. Her skin tingled and her face grew flushed.

Focus.

She didn't dare take another pill, not knowing the effects of a stronger dose on her driving.

She pressed on the accelerator. The faster she got home, the more likely she could stop her panic from rolling over her. The home on the ridge overlooking a lake was her safe place. It always had been.

Gripping the steering wheel tighter, she trained all her attention on the quickly disappearing yellow line in the middle of the road, separating the oncoming traffic from her little car. The snowplows hadn't been out yet.

She swallowed hard, then wiped one sweaty hand then the other on her coat.

"You can do this." She glanced in her rear-view mirror. No one else was on the road.

A rumble made her tighten her grip on the steering wheel. Road noise. It was just road noise.

Thump, thump, thump.

"Oh, come on, what is that?" Violet glanced at the dash. The low tire pressure indicator for the rear passenger tire was on. Her heart sank and heat flooded her face. "Oh, you have to be kidding me."

A hard knot formed in her stomach.

She squinted out the windshield, trying to figure out exactly where she was, but knowing the closest gas station was in town, a mile away or so. Could she drive on a flat tire? Even if she damaged the rim, she could afford repairs.

She pressed the accelerator, thinking that the closer she was to town when her vehicle became undrivable, the better.

Thump, thump, thump.

The sound grew louder. Her vision tunneled.

"What am I going to do?" she muttered.

A pop sounded and the steering wheel yanked to the right. Despite her efforts to gain control of the car, it swerved off the road.

"Oh, no—"

The steering wheel shook violently under her grasp. Her little red car bumped off the road. A scream ripped from her throat as bare branches smacked the windshield and sides of her car.

CHAPTER 3

Theo hopped into his truck and headed toward town. His five-year-old son had talked him into picking him up from kindergarten today after complaining the bus was too loud and the trip was too long. Theo agreed to pick him up *this* time, but that was it. Liam had to learn to be a big boy and ride the bus from now on.

Theo smiled to himself, realizing Liam knew as well as he did that today was *not* going to be the last time he picked him up from school. He'd do anything for his son, especially because Theo remembered the long bus ride home himself when he was a kid, with all the noise and diesel fumes. And the bigger kids trying to prove how tough they were. But they'd soon learned not to mess with Theo Cooper. No one got into Theo's face without getting a bloody nose for their troubles.

Looking back, he was never proud of himself for always being in trouble. He hoped he could guide his own son toward being a productive, God-fearing adult without repeating all his mistakes.

Now that Theo was back in Liam's life, he was going to

make up for lost time. And if he had known what was going on with Liam's mother, he would have come home much sooner.

As the familiar tune to some country song played over the radio, Theo's thoughts drifted to his meeting with Violet Jackson. Her hair was still long, dark and silky. He remembered the feel of it as it brushed against his cheek when they danced at the prom. Yet her face was narrower now. Mature. And still as beautiful as ever. But underneath, he sensed she was waging a battle of some sort. She'd held her coat as if it were a security blanket. He wondered if the anxiety that plagued her as a teen was still affecting her as an adult, but he wouldn't dare ask. Not immediately. He knew how private she was.

Or maybe he had completely misread her.

He ran a hand across his stubbled jaw and adjusted the wipers on his truck. Snow sure was coming down. A significant snowfall in early November didn't bode well for the rest of the winter.

Sighing heavily, he thought back to their casual conversation. She'd deflected his question on *why* she was interested in the job. Was she bored? Then he laughed to himself. How bored did a person have to be to take a bookkeeping job? Maybe she was just doing Isaac a favor, since the caretakers at her mother's house were good friends with his father. He supposed he'd have time to ask her these questions now that she'd be working for him.

Working for me. The notion made him laugh. The class valedictorian working for the class juvenile delinquent.

Sure, they had gone to the prom together, but that had been a mistake. Or maybe trusting his ex Jenny to keep her mouth shut had been a bigger one.

Theo turned up the speed on his windshield wipers yet again as the snow grew more steady. He slowed his vehicle so as not to slide through the intersection. The back end of his truck fishtailed even as he took the turn slowly. The plows had better hurry up and salt the roads or the ditches would be littered with cars.

Up ahead, he noticed tire tracks in the freshly fallen snow and then deep ruts veering off the road. *Exactly what I feared.* He slowed and squinted through his windshield wipers and the gathering snow. His heart hammered in his chest. The back end of a little red sports car stuck out of an overgrown cluster of bushes with bare branches. Narrowing his gaze, he jammed on the brakes, skidded a few feet before pulling over. He slammed the gear into park and turned on his flashers. He jumped out and ran toward the car.

"Violet!"

The wind whipped around his ears and fear fisted in his gut. Theo slipped between the prickly branches and the side of her car. He pried open the car door as far as he could against the stiff branches.

Through the opening, Violet turned to look at him, an unreadable expression on her face.

"Are you hurt?" He couldn't see any obvious injuries.

Violet shook her head. Her lips trembled. "I'm fine. I don't know what happened. I mean, I think I got a flat. I should have pulled over right away, but thought I could make it to a gas station."

"Can you stand?" Theo pushed his back against the branches, forcing them out of the way while he pulled her door open wider and offered his hand. A sharp branch poked him in the back of the neck and he hid a wince. Violet placed her cold, trembling hand in his and he helped her ease out of the vehicle.

He held the branches back so she wouldn't get scraped. They slid along the side of the car and reached the back of the vehicle. She looked exceptionally pale.

"You want to wait in my truck while I check your tire?"

"I'm fine." She crossed her arms over her middle and shuddered.

"You'd be warmer in my truck."

"I'm fine," she repeated, the wind whipping color back into her cheeks.

"Sounds like you had a tire blowout. Do you have a spare?" Without waiting for an answer, Theo tapped her trunk, then walked to check the other side of the vehicle. His boots crunched on the newly fallen snow. The rubber on the back passenger tire had fallen away from the rim. Theo shoved the branches out of the way and crouched by the tire for a closer inspection. He pulled out a long screw and held it up. "I think I found the culprit."

Violet stared down at him with her arms tightly crossed over her chest. "I wonder where I picked that up."

Theo inspected the screw. "We use these fasteners at work." He narrowed his gaze. "Not sure why it was in the parking lot, but that would be my best guess."

He angled his head and studied the tire closer. He tugged out another screw and saw the heads of two more poking out of the tire.

"What?"

He stood and held out his palm with the two screws. "There are at least two more in your tire. I'm surprised you got this far before getting a flat."

Violet blinked slowly. "Maybe someone dropped a box of screws in your parking lot and I ran over them?" Something akin to hope flashed in her eyes.

He lifted his brow. "You'd have to be mighty unlucky to have four screws penetrate the rubber of one tire."

She lifted her perfectly manicured eyebrows as if to say, *Yeah, well...*

He shook his head. "My guess...someone did this on purpose."

Violet bowed her head. Snowflakes dotted her dark brown hair and the ones that melted left tiny drops. She muttered something he couldn't make out. He took a step to stand directly in front of her. He thought back to their history. *Her* history. Everything she had shared with him as a teenager.

"Do you know who might have done this?"

Tiny stars danced in Violet's line of vision in competition with the big flat flakes falling from the sky. She tried to blink back her dizziness, but feared it was a losing battle. Suddenly she had the urge to flee. But where was she going to go? She was stuck in a field out in the middle of nowhere with a flat tire.

Her temporary respite from panic was ebbing away.

Theo's question bounced around her brain. *Do you know who might have done this?*

The look of hatred in Elmer's eyes from earlier today immediately came to mind. Could he have done this?

No...

The Amish were a gentle people. Right?

However, when you believed with all your heart that you had a stalker at age twelve, you learned to watch people. Study them. Read them. Intuit their intentions.

Elmer was an angry man. A very angry man.

"*Do you* know who might have wanted to drive these screws into your tire?" Theo asked again when she didn't respond.

Violet looked up slowly, meeting the concern in his eyes. She hitched her shoulders, trying to act nonchalant, not to read the very worst into this situation. Hunters Ridge was supposed to be her safe place.

Nothing was supposed to hurt her here.

She cleared her throat. "Did you see anyone around the parking lot who didn't belong?" She studied his face, but it was obvious he hadn't seen any more than she had. And she didn't want to cause any trouble for Elmer and the Grabers if she was just being paranoid. "I don't know who would do this."

Violet touched the smooth metal of the trunk, trying to ground herself in the moment. Not allow her thoughts to race and spiral into a domino of panicky emotions, one falling on top of the other until they crushed her lungs, making it difficult to breathe.

Stop.

Deep breath.

She exhaled on a cloud of frozen vapor.

The car has a flat and it's stuck in the snow and there's no way to get out of here that won't take a really long time and meanwhile Theo Cooper is going to see me have an all-out panic attack and I'm going to embarrass myself and I won't be able to work for him because he'll see that I haven't changed. That I'm still weak and crazy and unable to control my emotions.

Stop. Violet made a fist and dug her nails into the palm of her hand. Then she tapped each finger with her thumb. It helped a little.

I'm not alone. Theo will help me. I won't be stranded for long. I can handle this.

A more rational voice tried to tamp down her growing fear, but it was a mighty battle.

Theo flipped back the carpet in her trunk to expose the spare tire. He stopped what he was doing and looked at her, *really* looked at her. He took her gently by the elbow. "Please, let's get in my truck. Your lips are turning blue. And I really need you to not get sick because my books are a mess." A twinkle lit his eyes, as he obviously tried to lighten the mood.

Violet bit her lower lip, as if that would put some color into them.

Too cold to argue, she allowed him to guide her over to his truck, her dress shoes making a crunching sound on the snow and the frozen earth beneath. He helped her into his truck, then jogged around to get in his side. He fired up the engine and turned the heater on full blast.

"Give it a second. We'll have hot air pumping out of here in no time." He adjusted the heating vents toward her.

"Thanks." The warm air felt heavenly on her frozen face.

"Would you have a problem if we left your car here? I'll call a friend of mine and he can tow it into town for you. Even if I change the tire, it'll be tough to get the car out of the field."

"That would be great." She yanked on the seatbelt and drew it across her body and snapped it into place, already feeling calmer knowing that she'd be getting home sooner, rather than later.

"My sister Olivia is a deputy. I can call her and report the incident."

Violet waved her hand, not wanting to make this something it wasn't, remembering the curt interrogation of the New York City policeman who let it be known he had better things to do than respond to calls about imagined stalkers from privileged kids who had probably watched too many Lifetime movies.

Her mother wasn't much help either, claiming that all the attention from strangers was a small price to pay for wealth and fame.

"Maybe I ran over the screws. I don't want to cause a fuss." She smiled weakly, hardly convincing herself, much less him. At age twelve, her stalker might have been imagined, but the resulting panic attacks were very real, leading her mother to eventually send her off to a quiet house in the country to attend high school and recover away from the spotlight. It had been exactly what Violet needed to rebalance her world after a couple years of looking over her shoulder. Her mother seemed to enjoy not having her worrywart daughter dragging her down.

But there had been nothing imagined about Abby's vicious murder in Violet's New York City apartment less than two months ago. A random attack, they said. A botched robbery. Not targeted.

Not a stalker.

Violet wasn't so sure.

Abby's death had been a reality, so why was Violet still reluctant to report her new concerns to law enforcement? She blinked away her dizziness and reached out and redirected the heating vent away from her face. The horrific memory of her dear friend's lifeless body welled up and crashed over her, threatening to forever trap her in a world of doubt, fear and anxiety. *That's* why she wasn't quick to report her flat tire as more than an accident. Her panic made her doubt her own fears. Violet ran her fingers through her damp hair, wondering if she'd ever get her head on straight.

"I won't call my sister at the sheriff's department right away, but I think you should consider it."

"Sure." Violet forced a cheeriness she didn't feel into her tone. Right now her focus was single-minded: home.

Theo dialed a number, then whispered to her. "Do you have a preference where your car gets towed? I know a mechanic in town."

"No preference." *Just hurry up, please.* She'd agree to anything right now if it meant getting home. The thought of being stranded on the side of the road was one of her panic triggers.

Now here she was *really* stranded and *really* panicking. Funny how that worked.

Theo ended the call. "A tow truck's on its way." He seemed to look right through her. "I gave him the location. The car should be fine here. I'll tuck the keys under the visor. Mind if we pick up my son? He'll be waiting for me at school."

A rush of relief lifted her spirits. "Of course. Of course. I'm sorry if I made you late." She tugged on her seatbelt, trying to ignore the cold, icy pulse of adrenaline coursing through her veins. "I didn't realize you had a son." Her gaze drifted to his left hand. No ring. She wondered what that meant. Maybe nothing. Some guys didn't wear rings.

"Yeah," Theo said, an air of pride in that single word, "Liam's in kindergarten. He normally takes the bus to work after school, but he convinced me to pick him up today. He has me wrapped around his finger. Let me take care of the keys and then we'll get out of here."

"Sounds good."

On the drive into town, Violet didn't ask any questions about Liam's mother because it wasn't her business. Right now, her focus was on getting through this panic attack. Thankfully, her symptoms began to subside.

An Amish gentleman bundled against the cold tipped his hat as he drove his buggy along the edge of the road in the other direction. Theo nodded in return. He put on his directional and turned into the loop in front of the school. A bus pulled away and a young woman stood holding a little boy's hand. Her face brightened when she noticed Theo.

Theo reached for the door handle. "I'll be right back." He climbed out of the truck and jogged around the front. The little boy broke free from the woman and wrapped his dad in a big hug. Violet's heart did a little flutter. She wasn't exactly sure why.

Theo got his son settled in the back seat, then climbed in behind the steering wheel.

"Liam, this is my friend Miss Violet."

"Hi, Miss Violet," a sweet voice floated up from the back seat.

"Hello, Liam." She shifted in her seat to see him better.

An oversized backpack sat beside him with some completely unfamiliar cartoon character staring back at her. She remembered liking Scooby-Doo at that age, but her mother insisted her backpack be the latest brand name, along with her coat and shoes. And they always had to match. Appearances were everything when your mother was a famous movie star and entrepreneur.

"How was school?" Violet didn't have much experience with kids, but she figured that was a pretty standard question.

"I had a long day." Liam gave a world-weary sigh.

She turned and met Theo's gaze. She couldn't help but smile.

"I've had a long day, too," Violet commiserated. "A very long day."

CHAPTER 4

*T*he engine on Theo's truck shifted into low gear as it climbed the hill leading to Violet's home. He had never been officially invited to the sprawling home on the ridge, but he had been here once and it wasn't for prom. Violet had insisted on meeting him in town that night.

As teenagers, he and his friends had come up here late one night after drinking and tried to break into the garage. According to the rumor mill, Violet Jackson was actually the daughter of the famous movie star Jacque Caldwell, not that anyone believed that to be true at the time. Turns out, joke was on them. Anyway, a limited edition Ferrari had been parked in the garage. Fortunately for all parties involved, the house was secured like Fort Knox, preventing him from adding grand larceny to his rap sheet of petty teenage offenses.

From the back seat, Liam asked, "Did you ever sled down this hill? I bet you would go really fast."

"You might end up in the lake," Theo said.

"No, I never tried sledding down the hill," Violet said. "I did learn how to snowshoe, though. Haven't done it in a while. I've been too busy with work and I've kinda gotten soft when it comes to snow."

As the house came into view, Liam gasped in the back seat. "Are these apartments?"

"No, it's my house. Well, technically, my mother's house."

"It's gi-*gan*-tic."

Theo reached over the seat and wiggled his son's knee and laughed. "It is pretty gi-nor-mous."

"Yeah, gi-*nor*-mous," his son repeated.

Theo parked in the driveway between the ornate entryway and the fountain. The water had been shut off for the winter but the remaining water had pooled and frozen in the basin.

Theo shifted in the truck to face her after he parked. "Are you sure you don't want me to call my sister and report the vandalism to your car?"

"Is Aunt Olivia going to arrest a bad guy?" Liam asked.

"First we have to see if there was a bad guy. Miss Violet had a screw in her tire."

"Hmm…" Liam scooted back in the seat and moved to his side window and pressed his nose against it. "Why are there two doors on the house?"

Theo hitched a shoulder and mouthed, "Sorry" to Violet.

"Nothing to be sorry about. It is a pretty big house."

"How many kids do you have?" Liam asked. "You could have like a gazillion kids in a house this big."

"Liam," Theo scolded his son, realizing he wasn't going to be able to discuss anything of significance with his precocious son in the back seat who thought nothing of sharing whatever popped into his brain.

Violet held up her hand. "It's okay. I don't have any kids. I'm not even married." She exaggerated the last bit, as if it would be hard to believe she hadn't taken a walk down the aisle.

Theo found himself waiting to see if she was going to reveal anything more about herself. Perhaps a boyfriend? But he didn't dare ask. Probing questions were cute from a five-year-old. From a grown man, not so much.

The sound of crunching footsteps drew his attention to the front door. Betty Weaver, the caretaker, was standing on the porch, waving to them. Theo pushed the down button on the window control and returned her greeting.

"I saw the 'Cooper and Sons' on the side of the truck. How are you, Theo?"

"Great. Just dropping Violet off." He figured he could allow her to explain about the flat tire.

"Something wrong with her car?" The way she said it suggested she feared something more was wrong. He wondered if Violet was going to confide in him.

Violet opened her door and climbed out. As she picked her steps carefully so as not to fall on the icy driveway, he could hear her telling Betty that she'd had a flat. Violet obviously didn't want to alarm her by telling her that someone had intentionally flattened her tire and she had run off the road as a result.

"Is that Liam's nose I see pressed against the back window?" Betty smiled brightly and pulled her plain blue sweater sleeves down over her hands and shuddered against the cold. His father had told him Betty and Isaac Weaver had grown up Amish, married, then left the faith, finding employment doing odds and ends until eventually settling in at the big house on the hill, as people in town tended to call it. Although Betty didn't dress in Amish attire, she did dress simply.

"Oh, yeah. He thinks you live in a castle." Theo glanced into the back seat and said to his son, "Say hello to Mrs. Weaver." The Weavers had been good to his family when his father fell ill, bringing food and well wishes to the house.

But Theo had never brought his son to their home until now.

Liam scooted forward and stuck his head between Theo's seat and the window. "Hello." Then to his dad, as if he had something to do with it, "It's cold out there."

"I hope your dad is doing well," Betty hollered, holding her collar closed at the neck.

"I imagine he's doing better in Florida than we are right now."

Betty smiled as Violet reached the porch and turned around. "Thanks for the ride."

"Do you need a ride to work tomorrow?" Theo asked.

"I can figure something out."

"I don't mind. Besides, you're doing me a big favor by taking this job. I know it's not exactly going to be a challenge for you."

Violet hitched a shoulder. "It gets me out of the house. And yeah, a ride would be great." She sounded resigned as she lifted her hand to wave goodbye.

"See you tomorrow." Theo slid the window back up.

"That lady seems nice." Liam scrambled back into his car seat and buckled himself in.

Theo studied his son in the rear-view mirror. His brown eyes were wide with wonder as he took in the huge estate. Theo could relate. Even at his age, he was still impressed by the amount of wealth that could afford a place like this.

A knot tightened in his gut. Violet Jackson was so far out of his league.

Easy, buddy. She's only working for you. Doing a favor for Dad.

Still, the thought of having someone with Violet's credentials organizing his books brought back all those crushing feelings of when he was a kid and had to act like a tough guy. No one mocked you for not having a mom if they thought you were going to crack their skull for being stupid enough to mention it.

Theo winked at his son in the review mirror. Liam tried to wink back, but instead smooshed up his entire face and lifted a corner of his lip. Theo laughed at his failed attempt.

A hint of regret threaded its way into this simple moment. Theo'd never be able to look at his son's face without remorse for missing countless moments during the first five years of his life.

Other than the occasional weekend and a few weeks a year, Theo had been an absent father. He thought he had been doing the right thing by pursuing a career in the army, even if it meant leaving his son behind. It wasn't until he returned home for good after his father's heart attack that Theo fully engaged in young Liam's life. He wasn't proud of the fact, but he'd make up for it. Especially now that Liam's drug-addicted mother had proved unreliable.

"You buckled in?"

"Got it, Dad."

Theo stretched between the front seats to check the latch on his car seat. He'd never let anything happened to Liam.

Violet stepped into the foyer of the mansion she'd called home from the age of fourteen until she went away to college. The familiar scent of lavender and Betty's home cooking always made her feel like she had just emerged from a yoga class, all loose and de-stressed.

She'd been back to Hunters Ridge a handful of times over the past nine years, but only for a day here and there. And as life got busier, the visits were fewer and farther in between.

But after Abby's death, Violet had returned to try to reset her life. Find the peace and calm she had found after her mother had purchased this house in the middle of nowhere in the hopes of keeping Violet out of the spotlight as she struggled with anxiety. At Violet's request, her mother had changed her daughter's last name and left her here under the care of Betty to live her life and go to school free from a stalker no one could prove was out there.

After her mother had gotten Violet settled, she'd promised she'd be back every weekend, but being a movie star and using that power to brand her own clothing line and home goods wasn't a traditional job. Eventually, Jacque Caldwell didn't even pretend to be trying to clear her schedule to visit her daughter in that dreadfully boring small town, instead leaving Violet in the care of Betty Weaver.

Violet did white-knuckle it to New York City every so often, but mostly she stayed where she felt safe. Even though she missed her mom, Violet loved Betty. Where her mother was pushy, vain and judgmental, Betty was accepting and so calm. It went a long way toward Violet's recovery from anxiety.

"How did your day go?" Betty asked, holding out her hand for Violet's coat. Violet couldn't help but smile. Sweet Betty was almost seventy, but her smooth skin made her look years younger. Violet often wondered if her lifestyle kept her young. Her mother's housekeeper seemed to take everything in stride.

"I got it." Violet slipped the coat from Betty's grasp and the prescription bottle fell out of her coat pocket, hit the tile floor and the lid popped off, spilling the little pills. One rolled across the floor and disappeared under the table.

Heat immediately infused Violet's cheeks. The words *They're not mine* sprang to mind, but died on her lips.

Betty bent over and picked up the bottle. She glanced at it, then looked up at Violet. "What is this? Who is Zoe

35

Michaels?" Betty's face collapsed in a frown. "Let me guess, one of your mother's assistants."

Violet didn't bother to argue.

Folding the coat over her arm, Violet backed up and sat on the bottom step of the sweeping staircase. She watched, immobile, as Betty picked up each pill and put them in the container. She found the lid and the last pill under the hall table. Snapping the lid back on, Betty sat down next to Violet. "You don't need these." But she handed the bottle to Violet. Betty wasn't one to tell her what to do.

Violet accepted the bottle and stared at it through a watery gaze. "I keep telling myself that. They're my security blanket."

"Remember what you were going through when you first came here as a teenager?"

Violet laughed. "How could I forget? I was a stress ball."

"And you came out of it. With a lot of hard work. You left here and went to college, went to work for your mom. You've been doing great things."

Violet held out her hand, fingers wide. "And it all slipped through my fingers."

"Don't you think anyone who's been through what you've been through would need a minute to regroup?"

"It's taking longer than a minute."

"You'll get better." Betty squeezed her hand. "With more hard work."

Violet scratched her head. "I'm not so sure."

"That's how you felt then, too. But you're not that scared little girl. You're so much older and wiser now. It won't be as hard to work through your feelings. You have the tools."

Violet shook her head. "I can't get Abby out of my mind. If I had been home. It would have been me."

"But it wasn't. God spared you. God rest Abby's soul, but her death is not your fault."

"But if she hadn't been there..." She ran a finger under her nose. "Her family blames me."

"They're hurting. They'll come around. The Amish believe in forgiveness."

The hatred in Elmer's eyes was etched in her memory. Four fasteners had been driven into her tire shortly after she visited Abby's family's home. "I'm not so sure." And even if they did forgive her, how could she ever forgive herself?

"Even if they forgot what they have been taught and don't forgive you, you can't let that stop your recovery. You can't continue like this."

"I know."

Betty slapped her thighs and stood, resolved to move past this. "So tell me, how did things go today? I see Theo is as handsome as ever." Her eyes traveled to the gallery of photos on the hall table. She plucked a photo from behind a professional shot of Violet's mother at some award ceremony holding a statue of some sort.

Violet stood and took the silver frame from Betty. Theo had his hands on her waist and his chin playfully resting on her shoulder. Her head had been tipped back in laughter when the photographer snapped the prom photo. The night had been magical until Jenny, Theo's old girlfriend, had cornered her in the bathroom.

Violet set the frame back down. "You've kept up with him all these years. You knew he had a son."

"You forget how small this town is. Isaac and I are friendly with his father."

She debated asking the question, but finally did. "Who did he marry?"

Betty lifted her eyebrows, a twinkle in her eyes. "He's not married." She patted Violet's hand. "Now if you're wondering who Liam's mother is, that's an entirely different question."

She raised her eyebrows and gave Violet a knowing glance. "Jennifer Koch."

"Really?" Violet tried to hide her disbelief, but why should that surprise her? Why should anything surprise her? Theo had been dating Jenny, and they'd broken up two months before prom. They obviously had gotten back together. Jenny had said they always would.

"I don't believe they're still together." It was as if Betty was reading her mind.

Violet opened the closet at the bottom of the stairs. She dropped the bottle of pills back into her pocket and hung up her coat. "If you're hinting that I should date Theo, you're barking up the wrong tree.

"I would never suggest that."

Violet rolled her eyes as if to say, *Of course not.* Hadn't Betty orchestrated the whole prom fiasco? To be fair, none of them could have foreseen the fiasco part.

"Dinner will be ready in ten minutes."

The aroma of sauce in the kitchen made Violet's stomach rumble. "Smells great. But you don't have to make dinner every night for me. I'm a big girl. I can fend for myself."

"It's my job."

Despite having been away from Hunters Ridge for years, Jacque kept the Weavers on the payroll to maintain the house. Violet always considered it a sign of her mother's gratitude for taking care of her daughter so she didn't have to. Her mother did have a heart, deep down.

Betty reached up and touched her cheek. "I enjoy cooking for you. You've been gone too long." The older woman wrapped Violet in a warm hug. "That's my girl. You'll be back to yourself in no time."

After her whirlwind of emotions today, Violet was beginning to wonder if she'd ever feel like herself again.

CHAPTER 5

"W e won't be long," Theo told Liam as they pulled up in front of the trailer office at Cooper and Sons after they dropped Violet off at her house. Liam had chatted about the size of the house for most of the drive. Theo hated to think his son was so impressed by wealth. Or maybe he was overthinking it. Any five-year-old would be amazed by the big house on the hill.

Man, he was still surprised by the house. Who needed that much space?

Theo parked the truck in the lot and sighed. The snow clouds had cleared and a hint of purple and pink sky remained on the horizon. Days had grown both short and cold. He sensed a long winter on the horizon, but the thought of working with Violet cheered him.

"Can I play a video game?" Liam scooted across the back seat and opened the door.

"Maybe one."

Theo had set up a couch and TV with video games at one end of the trailer-slash-office for the days when his son got stuck hanging out at work with him. Before Liam started kindergarten, he had spent most of his days with his grand-mother, Jenny's mom. But now that Theo lived in Hunters Ridge and Liam was in school, the little boy took the bus home to the lumberyard. Some days, Liam hung out here, and other times his Aunt Mandy, Jenny's sister, picked up Liam to play with his cousin, Noah. Lately Jenny had been coming along with her sister, participating in limited super-vised visitation as per the court's instructions.

Theo shuddered to think what might have happened to Liam if Theo hadn't returned to Hunters Ridge after his father's heart attack. It still made him hot to think Jenny had been stoned most afternoons while Liam made himself dinner with whatever was in the pantry and put himself to bed.

Often hungry.

Jenny had gone through rehab and vowed to stay clean. Since a kid needed his mom, Theo was willing to work with her and was grateful the court authorized supervised visits. This whole mess made Theo realize he should have been more selective about who he got involved with. But he had been young and foolish.

After maturing and serving in the military, Theo knew two things without a doubt: he'd never regret Liam and he'd never leave him again.

"We won't be long. I need to wrap up a few things and then we'll get dinner."

"Pizza?" Liam asked enthusiastically as he raced up the metal steps leading to the trailer, the lights on his sneakers blinking.

Liam tousled his son's hair. "Don't you ever get sick of pizza?"

"Nope," he said, his tone an equal mix of *no way* and *you have to be kidding me.*

"I'll make us chicken and broccoli tonight. You have to eat healthy sometimes."

"*Bleck*." His son stuck his tongue out as Theo reached around him to push open the door, surprised to find it unlocked.

He ushered his son into the office and heat poured out to greet them. Theo's shoulders slightly sagged when he saw his cousin, Chad, sitting at the desk squinting at the computer screen. Theo had hoped to zip in and out, avoiding a long discussion with Chad. His cousin loved to talk, which made him a great salesman, but talking meant time, something which Theo didn't feel like wasting.

Not tonight.

Chad looked up and smiled his greeting. Chad and Theo grew up together, only a year apart. His cousin held out his arm to give Liam a fist bump. "How's it going, little man?" Chad stuck out his lower lip and let out a long breath, blowing his long bangs from his forehead. The rest of his hair was generally unkempt and hung down to his shoulders. If hippies were still a thing, Chad would have fit right in. People were drawn to his easygoing nature. And his casual wardrobe didn't seem to pose a problem when selling outdoor play sets.

"Good. Except I don't like chicken."

Chad closed down a few screens and blinked away from the computer screen. A thin line marred his forehead. "I thought you ate a consistent diet of chicken nuggets. What happened, my man?"

Liam giggled. "Not chicken nuggets. I love nuggets. Dad wants to make chicken. The real kind."

Chad raised his eyebrows in understanding. "Your dad is one mean dude."

Liam shook his head then jumped over the back of the couch facing the corner with the TV and gaming system.

41

"Have you ever heard of walking around the couch and sitting down like I've asked you?"

Chad looked up at Theo. "Don't be so hard on him. He's a kid. We did far worse stuff than jumping over the back of a couch." He made a face, a mix between commiserating with Liam and suggesting he was about to share a story or two.

Theo tipped his head slightly in the direction of his son. Liam didn't need an earful about his father's wild past. Theo had to constantly remind his cousin to watch what he said because being just one year older had made Chad the witness to a lot of crazy stuff. It was hard enough showing up on the scene when his son was already five—even without someone always undermining him.

Chad held up his palm as if to say, *What does it really matter?* But to Theo it did matter. He wanted to do right by this little boy who had already suffered so much disruption in his young life.

"You plan on working for a while? I only swung by to do a few things and lock up." Theo dropped down in the chair Violet had sat in a few hours earlier. He still had a hard time wrapping his head around the idea that they were going to be working together.

"I'm pretty much done with my paperwork for the night." Chad tapped the scraps of paper in front of him.

"Good news," Theo said, straightening his back. "I've got some help with that."

Chad lifted a bushy eyebrow. "Violet Jackson actually accepted the job? I thought she'd take one look at our small operation and realize we're small potatoes." The implication that either the job or Theo wasn't worth her time rubbed him the wrong way, but he refused to argue about it.

"Apparently, she's in Hunters Ridge for a few months and was in the market for a side job."

"The rich girl who lives in the big house on the hill needs

a side job?" Annoyance edged his cousin's tone. "I thought she agreed to the interview to humor your dad because her maid or something is friends with him. She probably makes more in a month than our business sees in a year." He made a noise with his lips. "Ten bucks she's gone in a week."

"That will be one week of receipts we won't have to organize."

Chad leaned back in the chair and crossed his arms over his chest, a smug look on his face. "When does she start?"

"Tomorrow morning. I figured it's a short-term gig. She'll get us caught up. Set us up with accounting software, make it easier for us to track our expenses and income. Not like Dad's ledger. We'll keep on top of it once we're organized."

"I guess pigs do fly," Chad muttered, then reached out and wiggled the mouse on the computer. He squinted at the screen.

"Hey…" Theo leaned forward, resting his forearms on his thighs. "Violet got a flat after leaving here this afternoon. She had at least four screws jammed in her tire. Did you see anything suspicious today out in the parking lot? She ended up with a blown tire and lost control of her vehicle. Had to have her car towed out of a field."

"You have to be kidding me. Is she okay?"

"She's fine. Just shaken up." He straightened and reached into his jacket pocket and pulled out his cell phone. "I want to put a call in to Olivia. Just so the sheriff's department has a heads-up." He hoped Violet didn't mind.

"Yeah sure. Good idea. What kind of car does she drive? I can ask around. See if anyone saw something." Chad sounded incredulous.

"It had to be intentional. Four screws. Like the ones in our kits." He glanced over his shoulder, relieved to find his young son totally engrossed in his game and not listening to the adult conversation.

"I tell you, though, Violet Jackson has had a tough few months."

Theo stopped dialing his sister's phone number and stared at his cousin. "What are you talking about?"

"You didn't hear?" There was an air of disbelief in his cousin's tone.

"Tell me what it is and I'll tell you if I've heard." A slow, steady pulse grew louder in his ears.

"You don't know the reason she returned to Hunters Ridge?"

He slowly shook his head, trying to remember what he had heard, but until his father had called him from Florida, telling him Violet could pinch hit and organize their books, he hadn't thought of her in years.

Well, that wasn't completely true.

"I read it online. She came home late one night and found her friend Abigail Graber murdered in her kitchen."

"The Amish girl who left here to work within the Jacque Caldwell organization?"

"Yeah, how about that for a welcome to the world? She had her head—"

Theo held up his hand and jerked his chin toward his son on the couch. "Another time."

"Of course. Sorry." Chad closed the folder and pushed back from the desk. "I'm going to take off. You good here?"

"I'm all set. Night."

Liam turned around with a glazed look in his eyes. "Night, Chad."

Chad ruffled Liam's hair, then with a yank at the door he left. "Don't work too hard."

Theo's gaze drifted to an animated character jumping up and down on the TV screen. "How about we get out of here, too?" Theo lost any motivation he had for work.

Liam tossed down the controller and jumped up on the

couch cushion. "Pepperoni and cheese?" The kid was persistent.

"Chicken and broccoli, remember?"

Liam groaned.

"Come on." Theo turned his back to the couch and glanced over his shoulder, holding out an arm. Taking the invitation, Liam dove onto his father's back. Theo made an exaggerated groan. "You're getting too big for this." Yet secretly, he hoped it would be a long time before that day came.

∾

The next morning, Violet hustled outside when she saw Theo's truck pull up in the circular driveway. She hopped into his truck and said a quick hello to Liam in the back seat. He muttered a quiet hello, but didn't look up from one of those handheld video games. Or was he playing on a smartphone?

Did five-year-olds have smartphones?

When Violet gave Theo a questioning gaze as to why he wasn't in school, Theo said, "Superintendent's day."

"Ah…" Violet buckled her seatbelt. Whatever that meant. "Makes me wonder how people who have children manage to work with all these school holidays."

"We do what we have to," Theo said matter-of-factly.

Violet was curious where Jenny was. Perhaps her job didn't allow her the flexibility to have a kid in tow.

They drove mostly in silence to the lumberyard, except for the occasional "Yes!" or "Awww…man" from the back seat. Apparently Liam was enjoying his game…or not, depending on the exclamation. When they arrived, Liam unbuckled and scooted toward the door.

"Here." Theo handed his son the keys to the trailer.

Liam bounded out the door. The sound of his feet clattered on the metal steps to the trailer. Violet had started to open the passenger door when Theo put his hand on her knee.

His touch caught her off guard. She glanced at his hand, then at him. Theo quickly pulled it away. "Sorry. Didn't mean to be rude. I want to talk to you a second. Away from Liam."

"Okay." Violet searched Theo's face. "What's up?"

"It's about Liam."

"Okay," she repeated, already figuring that much obvious.

"His mom, Jenny"—he widened his eyes as if to say it was obvious who his mother was—"is going to pick him up in a minute so he doesn't have to hang out in the trailer on his day off from school."

Violet's heart sank. Jenny wasn't exactly her favorite person. Nor did she want to let on that she and Betty had been talking about Jenny last night. Better for Theo to think she wasn't in the least interested in his personal life. She wasn't, was she?

"Oh." Her one-word replies made her feel foolish.

Theo glanced toward the trailer through the windshield, then back at Violet. Liam had managed to unlock the door and get inside. "His mom has had some issues and the courts only recently awarded her limited supervised visits."

"You don't sound happy about it." Her mind raced at all the possible reasons Jenny could have lost custody, but she wasn't comfortable asking, and quite frankly, it was none of her business.

Theo scrubbed a hand across his jaw. "It's been a long road, but Liam and I are finally doing great, just the two of us." His eyes moved around the interior of the truck, searching for the right words.

"It's really none of my business." Violet tried to let him off the hook. She wasn't sure why he felt the need to share this with her.

"I'd like you to know since you'll be working around here." He cleared his throat, obviously uncomfortable.

"Okay…" She forced a smile, not sure what to say.

"Liam's a really good kid, but every time he comes home from seeing his mom, he acts out. But she's his mom." There was a faraway quality to his voice. "A kid deserves to have a mom, right?"

If he was asking her for confirmation, he had picked the wrong person. Violet's mom provided well for her daughter but was mostly absent. Violet understood what it was like to be a kid who wanted her mom, but under very different circumstances. "I'm sorry. Can I help somehow?"

Theo turned to face her. "I don't mean to lay all this baggage on you, but I thought it would help if you knew what was going on."

"Sure." Violet kept her voice even as she reached for the door handle.

"And I know Jenny and you weren't exactly friends back in high school."

"Don't worry about it. High school was a lifetime ago."

"I appreciate your understanding."

"Sure thing." Violet held up her hand. "It's none of my business. I just work here." She tried to make light of the situation. Then she cocked her head, noticing the flicker of sadness in his eyes. "Would you rather Liam didn't go with her? Maybe you can sneak away from the office today and spend some time with your son on his day off."

A smile curved the corner of his mouth. "His aunt will be supervising the visit, so that means he gets to hang out with his cousin Noah. It'll be okay." Violet wondered if he added the last assurance for her or himself.

"Well, okay," Violet said, suddenly eager to get to work.

She pulled the door handle and for the first time since she had gotten into his truck this morning, she realized she hadn't been obsessing over any of her panic symptoms. She had made it all the way here without tingling fingers, light-headedness or a queasy stomach. A flicker of hope ignited in her heart.

With no medication.

Maybe this little job was exactly what she needed to get back her normal life. Get outside her head.

The sound of gravel crunching under tires drew her attention to a car pulling up alongside Theo's truck.

"Oh, that's Jenny. Let me go get Liam. He'll probably be disappointed he didn't have time for his game." Theo sounded resigned. He jumped out of the cab of the truck and jogged toward the trailer and disappeared inside.

Violet pushed open the passenger door and started to walk toward the trailer. The car door opened and the woman climbed out. After a cursory glance, Violet murmured politely, "Morning."

"You don't even recognize me, do you?" the woman said.

"How are you, Jenny?" Violet stopped and smiled, confirming that she did, indeed, know who she was.

A mocking smile flickered, then disappeared on the woman's face. "I'm sure you've heard all about me."

Violet sighed. "I'm just working here for a little while. That's all. Your business is your business."

"Well, I heard you were going to be working here. I wouldn't have believed it unless I saw it with my own eyes." She smirked. "New York City too stressful for you?" A hint of glee flashed through her eyes. This was a woman who took delight in someone else's suffering.

Not one to kick someone while they were down, Violet took the high road. "I'm in Hunters Ridge for a little bit and I heard the lumberyard needed some help."

"Yeah, sure." Venom and accusation dripped from the two simple words. Something flickered across her face that Violet couldn't read. "Why did you and Theo arrive at the same time?"

"He gave me a ride. I had a flat tire."

"Awww, too bad."

Violet returned the woman's tight smile. "Nice seeing you." She had dealt with a lot of sharks in the business world, but no one was as vicious as this woman who acted like she was still in high school and had it out for everyone.

Violet turned to leave, then Jenny called out to her. "Why are you even in Hunters Ridge? Really?"

"I'm…" Heat blossomed in Violet's face as she grew flustered at the woman's brazen tone. Squaring her shoulders, she ignored the panic tingling at her fingertips. "I'm doing Theo a favor."

"You're doing Theo a favor?" There was no shortage of disbelief in her tone.

Violet struggled to keep her face neutral. "Yes, I'm doing Theo a favor." Violet blinked slowly, suddenly feeling like she was fourteen again and being bullied in school, the new rich kid who apparently thought she was better than everyone else. Being different wasn't cool in high school. Everyone whispered about the new girl who lived in the big house on the hill. They wondered who she was and why she was in Hunters Ridge. It was a wonder *anyone* survived those years. But keeping her true identity secret meant keeping herself safe from her stalker.

A stalker who was never found.

Violet frowned and turned to walk into the trailer. "Nice to see you, but I have work to do."

"Wait." Jenny's urgent plea made Violet turn around. "I'm Liam's mom." There was a possessive quality to the woman's voice.

"Liam's a nice kid."

"He is. And I'm finally getting my life back. I'm finally getting visitation. I'm not going to have him calling someone else 'Mom.' *I'm* his mom."

Violet's pulse thrummed in her ears. "Don't be ridiculous. I'm just working here. You have nothing to worry about."

The sound of footsteps on the trailer steps drew Violet's attention. Liam ran past Violet and stopped short of his mom. Jenny glared at Violet for a full ten seconds before composing herself long enough to bend down and give her son a stiff-armed hug. The coolness broke Violet's heart.

"I'll see you later, Liam," Violet said.

"Bye, Miss Violet. Bye, Dad." Violet followed the little boy's gaze to his father standing on the stoop. Something on Theo's face, the set of his mouth, the hardness around his eyes, made Violet's heart break.

Not for the first time since she had accepted this accounting job for Cooper and Sons, Violet questioned her decision. She hated drama and the emotions it evoked.

Ever since Abby's death, Violet had far more drama than her nervous system could handle. She didn't need this, too.

CHAPTER 6

*T*heo waved to Liam as he drove away in the back seat of his aunt's car. A part of him hated to see Liam go off with his mother, a woman who had proven to be both untrustworthy and unreliable, but the courts had insisted she get visitation.

The other part knew how much a kid needed his mom. And Jenny genuinely seemed to be trying when she wasn't getting in her own way.

Violet brushed against him on the narrow stoop outside the trailer. For the briefest of moments, he had forgotten she was there. "Sorry. I had hoped you wouldn't have to deal with Jenny."

Violet lifted her eyebrows, but didn't say anything.

"She still says whatever's on her mind."

"I noticed."

"Whenever Jenny's around, there's drama." Embarrassment heated his cheeks. As much as he wanted to rise above bad choices—Jenny, not Liam—reminders kept finding him The man he was today would never have so thoughtlessly gotten involved with a woman like her. He'd never regret his son, he just regretted his wild days in his early twenties. But in the end, a kid needed the best shot at a stable home. Theo would do whatever it took to create that environment.

Theo opened his mouth, wanting to explain so much, but Violet lifted her hand and shook her head, letting him off the hook far easier than he deserved.

"She's apparently harboring some kind of grudge, but as far as I'm concerned, it's all in the past." Violet's tone was even.

"I was hoping to avoid a scene." Theo turned and opened the door to the trailer, holding it open for Violet. "I think I added fuel to the fire."

"I don't miss high school." Violet looked up at him with a spark in her eye as she brushed past him and went into the trailer.

"Yeah, me neither. But sometimes the choices we make when we're young and stupid haunt us into our adulthood."

"Don't worry about it." Violet stood in the middle of the trailer with her hands in her coat pockets, watching him with her beautiful brown eyes.

"I appreciate your understanding." Theo walked around to his side of the desk. The chair creaked under his weight as he flopped down. "I've created a mess, but I'm working hard to do better by my son." He drew in a deep breath and let it out. He leaned forward and pulled open the drawer. Then from inside the drawer, he pulled out a shoe box of receipts. "But that's not why you're here."

Violet slowly sat down on the chair on the opposite side of the desk. Not for the first time he hoped it didn't take long for her to get them organized. Because the longer she was around, the more he realized the type of woman he should have fallen for.

Well, he had fallen for her. He'd just messed it up royally.

Again, a decision of the young and stupid.

Violet worked on the buttons of her coat, then dropped it off her shoulders. Theo hustled out from behind the desk and took it from her. He hung it on a rack in the corner. "I apologize. We don't have much of an operation." He turned on the space heater and stared at it a second. "I'm not sure if this thing is working."

"I can always put my coat back on."

Theo bowed his head and rubbed the back of his neck. "This place is falling apart."

"How is business?"

"Pretty good. I'm sure you'll see that once you get into the numbers. But between my father's heart attack and my trying to get up to speed, we haven't been as organized as we should have been."

"How long has your cousin Chad been working here?"

"Since he dropped out of community college. His dad owned half the company with my dad before he died. So when he came back to Hunters Ridge, he helped out my dad. He's great with getting the play sets in the big box stores. He's a pretty good talker." He drummed his fingers on the desk. "I like to stay here and hold down the fort."

"And be here for Liam."

He nodded.

Violet crossed her arms over her chest. "Before your dad's heart attack, you had planned to make a career in the army?"

"Yes, that was my plan. I was stationed in Georgia. Mostly got home a weekend here, a weekend there. It wasn't until I came home after my dad's illness that I realized how much I was missing out on Liam's life. I thought providing money and the occasional visit was enough. I guess if you just keep living your life and don't stop to think, you don't realize you're on the wrong path."

Something flashed in her eyes and then disappeared

before it had a chance to register with him. Had he said something to offend her?

"Should we get started?" she asked, changing the subject abruptly.

Theo smiled. He pulled out a drawer and set a ledger on top of the shoe box. "My dad was old school, but he was organized. If there's something I can't answer, we can call him. He's more than happy to help."

"Good to know. I can help get you organized with software, if that's okay?" Violet leaned forward and flipped open to the first page of the ledger.

"Yes, definitely. Then we'll make sure we don't fall behind."

"Looks like we have a plan."

∾

Violet tucked her legs under her on the oversized chair she had pushed close to the fireplace in the sitting room off the kitchen. This had always been her favorite reading chair as a teenager. She had spent the latter half of the day dreaming about the time she'd be able to do this. The trailer never quite warmed up.

She shuddered, her body still trying to shake the cold that had seeped into her bones. She feared she was never going to get warm again. Her fingers had gone numb and she had insisted she bring a box of receipts home to do a little work to make headway. The faster she completed the job, the less time she'd have to spend in the cold trailer.

And with Theo.

The young man she had graduated from high school with was nothing like the man she was getting to know. He had a wonderful sense of humor, a kind heart, and he was a good father. Nothing like the stud muffin who had broken her trust and her heart on prom night.

Hadn't she agreed to go to prom with him because she had glimpsed the side of him she had witnessed today, even back then? But an eighteen-year-old Theo hadn't kept her secret.

No sense rehashing old news. It didn't matter then and it certainly didn't matter now.

A pity date, Jenny had told Violet when she found her in the bathroom outside the gymnasium that had been transformed into something out of the old movie *Grease*. It had been magical. Until Jenny trapped her in the bathroom stall, mocking her.

A spark crackled in the fire and an orange ember hit the screen. Violet's stomach twisted as she shoved away the memory.

Even if Jenny hadn't taken it upon herself to remind Violet of her place in the teenage pecking order, she and Theo would have never been anything more than prom dates anyway. Theo had taken her as a favor to his father, much as Violet was now doing their books as a favor to the Weavers. Such was life in small towns.

Theo's roots were firmly planted in Hunters Ridge. Her life was working for her mother. Making her proud. Proving that she wasn't that delicate flower who had to be tucked away in Hunters Ridge.

Yet here she was again.

Violet crossed her arms over her chest and shook away the thought. This was only temporary. She had to recharge and work through her panic. She'd recover.

She picked up the bowl of chili from the end table. Betty'd had some waiting on the stove for Violet when she got home because she and Isaac had gone bowling in town with friends.

The fire crackled and roared in front of her and for the first time in a long time, Violet had real hope. Her anxiety symptoms had been kept at bay for most of the day as she focused on the mundane task of organizing Cooper and Sons' books.

There was definite optimism that she'd move past this setback. And soon.

Violet finished her chili then set the bowl aside. Reaching down next to her, she picked up the box of receipts.

She flipped open her laptop and fired it up. She pulled out a receipt and flattened it out. A crackle drew her attention to the fireplace. Her mind drifted to Theo. Handsome Theo. He had been in and out of the trailer all day and she had enjoyed his company. It was such a leisurely pace compared to her usual hectic work life. She couldn't remember the last time she had sat in one place for such a long time. Her usual job required a lot of meetings and running around. Travel.

A twinge of anxiety bit at her fingertips at the thought of flying and she quickly pushed it aside.

She turned her focus to her work, squinting at an unreadable receipt. She fingered through the box and found some undated receipts. She laid them out on the chair next to her and drummed her fingers on them.

Talk about unorganized.

A creak drew her attention to the kitchen behind her. She froze and held her breath, waiting...hoping to convince herself it was just the wind outside.

Inwardly she rolled her eyes at herself. She was a big girl. She *could* stay home alone.

A shiver raced up her spine. A few feet away from the fire, her arms felt chilled. She got up and jogged up the sweeping staircase to her bedroom and returned with a thick sweater. She stuffed her arms in it and pulled it over her head and flopped back down in the chair. She picked up a receipt again and examined it. This was going to take far longer if she had to ask Theo or his cousin Chad about some of the receipts. Some were handwritten and others lacked a date.

Is this how small businesses operate?

Crazy.

She tipped her head back and let out a long sigh.

Creak.

She bolted upright and snapped her attention toward the kitchen. *Was* someone there?

"Betty?" she called, hating the squeak in her voice.

No answer.

Adrenaline surged through her veins. Her mind flashed to the night she had returned to her apartment late from work and found Abby dead in her kitchen. Pinpricks of panic washed over her scalp and arms. Her stomach knotted. She stood and slowly walked toward the sound, her mouth growing dry.

It's just the wind.

"Isaac?"

She let out a shaky breath.

A few feet from the entryway into the kitchen, a loud crash exploded, piercing her ears, and a piece of paper blew off the kitchen island and fluttered to her feet. Heart racing in her chest, she forced her leaden legs to keep walking into the kitchen. Her gaze landed on the French doors. One swung freely on its hinges in the wind. The dark, cold winter night lay beyond.

Betty and Isaac never used that entrance. They always came in through the mudroom. Their living quarters were through an enclosed hallway on that side of the house.

Terror sent goose bumps racing across her flesh. She ran to the door and slammed it shut and snapped the bolt into place. She stood off to the side, out of view of the French door, and peered out the windowpane. Her vision tunneled and she felt lightheaded. The path she had shoveled for herself to the wood pile on the edge of the porch was mostly clear. There were no discernible footsteps beyond her own.

Her fingers lingered on the wood frame of the door. Hadn't she shut the door all the way when she went out for wood for the fireplace? Had the wind blown it open?

Violet flattened herself against the wall. Tears burned the back of her eyes. Fear, disgust and loneliness swirled around her. She despised the person she had become. Afraid of her own shadow.

Her eyes snapped open. *What if someone is in the house?*

Violet ran back to the sitting room off the kitchen and grabbed her cell phone. She stared at the screen. As practical as it would be to call the sheriff's office, she couldn't get herself to do it.

Yet here she was, terrified to be alone.

What if no one believed her? What if there was nothing to believe?

She dragged a hand through her hair, suddenly fearing the repercussions of calling the sheriff's department more than she feared someone lurking in her house.

Her mother had demanded she go back to Hunters Ridge and pull herself together before she came back to work. Thinking someone was after you wasn't exactly pulling yourself together.

And she had been wrong before. Ruined reputations. Destroyed a big opportunity for her mother.

But why couldn't she shake this feeling someone was out there? Watching her.

Deep breath.

Her mind was a swirl of crazy, obsessive thoughts.

With her heart nearly racing out of her chest, she ran to the mudroom and yanked open the door to the garage. Maybe Betty and Isaac had returned. But the only cars in the garage were her sports car—repaired and dropped off by the garage —and her mother's rarely used SUV. Then she scurried around the downstairs, turning on all the lights. But even with the place blazing like some beacon guiding a spaceship in, she still felt lonely. Vulnerable. On the verge of an all-out stomach twisting, fingers tingling, vision tunneling panic attack.

She positioned herself in a corner of the kitchen, against the granite counter, with a set of butcher knives at her back. Not that she thought she could actually use a knife on someone.

Blood leaked out of Abby's neck into a pool of dark liquid on the slate floor.

Blinking rapidly, she tried to ignore the buzzing panic even as it morphed into an out of body experience. She *was* truly losing it. Truly.

Bracing her hands on the corner counter behind her, she stared at the French doors, convincing herself that she had been at fault. If the doors weren't latched just right, they swung open. She remembered her aching fingers carrying the wood in, her relief at dumping the logs by the fireplace. It wouldn't be unreasonable that she had carelessly closed the doors.

Swallowing hard, she squeezed her eyes shut and pressed her hand to her mouth. The idea of saying a prayer flitted across her brain and then disappeared. God had let her down a lot recently and she wasn't counting on Him to come to her in a pinch. He could have helped her get over these panic attacks already.

He could have saved Abby.

She shook the dark thoughts away.

Betty had taught her the calming effects of prayer and trusting in God.

Deep breath.

No, she had to count on herself. She closed her eyes and breathed in and out slowly. Her nerves tamped down just a fraction. Then an idea hit her.

She picked up her cell phone and dialed Theo's number, grateful he had given it to her for whatever. This felt like just such an occasion. She held her breath waiting for the line to connect.

"Hello," he said, his voice scratchy as if she had woken him up, but it was too early for him to have been in bed for the night.

"Hi, Theo. It's Violet."

"Hey, Violet. What's up? Is everything okay?" The concern in Theo's voice almost broke her down into tears.

"Um, I was working and I had a few questions about a couple receipts." She bowed her head, suddenly feeling silly. "It...um...can wait until tomorrow. I'm not sure why I called. I guess I thought we could go over a few things without any distractions."

"Okay. Why don't I stop over? It's early yet. I can explain those receipts."

Violet's gaze drifted to the wall clock. It was only seven o'clock, even though the black night made it seem later.

"You don't have to." She held up her hand as if he could see her. "It can wait. I'm not sure why I bothered you. Sometimes I get working and forget others have family. It can wait, really," she repeated, feeling herself blathering on.

I'm afraid to be alone doesn't seem like a grown-up excuse.

"You mind if Liam comes with me?"

"No, really. Tomorrow's fine. You probably need to get him to bed."

"Are you kidding? He'd love to go for a ride." Theo

laughed. The lightness in his voice already had Violet feeling better.

"Well, okay, if you're sure." Violet ended the call and felt more than a little silly. But she also felt relieved. The big house on the hill wouldn't seem so creepy if she had company.

CHAPTER 7

*T*heo heard several bolts scraping in the lock before Violet's face appeared in the crack of the open door. Concern creased the lines around her eyes. She pushed the door closed, releasing the chain, then opened it wide.

"Hi," she said, stepping back then holding out her hand. Her expression transformed into a cheery smile that seemed forced. "Come in."

Liam scooted in past him and craned his neck in awe as he took in the chandelier dangling from the two-story foyer. "This place is humongous inside, too."

Violet smiled brightly, genuinely this time. "My mom likes fancy things."

Lights blazed in every room. "Everything okay?" Theo whispered close to her ear to avoid scaring Liam. She smelled fresh, like soap with some floral scent. He took a step back, realizing he wasn't here on a date. He was here for professional reasons. To explain some receipts.

Violet shrugged and glanced up at him sheepishly, but she didn't answer. Their eyes locked and held.

Is she hiding something? Is she afraid of something? Had something else happened after her flat tire?

"Do you have toys?" Liam's earnest question broke the temporary spell. His son leaned on the wall outside an impressive office outfitted in mahogany paneling and rich leather. The room probably cost more than the house he grew up in. His son twisted his little body to peer into the room. Dirt caked the corner of his boot and Theo rushed over to slip them off, then stepped out of his own, leaving them lined up on the entryway rug. "Sorry about that."

"It's okay," Violet said, apparently sensing his unease. "You won't find any toys in that room. That's my mom's study."

Liam turned around, his face all scrunched up. "You live with your mom and dad?"

"It's my mom's house, but she's currently staying in her apartment in New York." Violet made a playful face at his son. "You live with your dad."

"Yeah, I'm five."

Violet tilted her head as if to say, *We all have to live somewhere.*

Theo was a little surprised with the easy banter between her son and Violet. Liam didn't always warm up to adults. And as far as Theo knew, Violet didn't have much experience with kids. It must be part of her professional nature to be able to adapt to situations, engage anyone in conversation.

"I have the receipts in the sitting room by the fireplace."

His feet felt cool through his socks as they crossed the tiled foyer.

She turned to Theo. "Is it okay if Liam watches TV?"

"I'm sure he'd love that."

"What do you like to watch on TV?" she asked.

"My dad doesn't let me watch much and when I'm at my mom's house she doesn't get many channels. Mostly talk shows with people yelling at each other." He shook his head, not even trying to hide his disapproval.

Smiling, Violet picked up the remote and aimed it at the TV. A popular news anchor on one of the 24/7 news stations filled the screen. She began flicking through the stations. "I'm not really sure what's on that's appropriate for a little boy—"

"I'm not a little boy!" Liam stuck out his lower lip, but she didn't miss the twinkle in his eyes. "I'm in kindergarten."

Violet lifted her palms in a surrender gesture. "My apologies, sir." She handed the remote to him as if she were offering him a prize on a silver platter. "Perhaps you'd like the remote."

Liam's eyes lit up. He took the remote, then climbed up onto the sofa across from the TV. He aimed the remote at the large screen, then settled on something on a kid-friendly station.

"You all set?" Theo asked his son. "Miss Violet and I have a little work to do."

"I'm good." Liam seemed transfixed by the cartoon characters dancing on the screen.

"I have my computer in the sitting room right over here." Violet led him to another sofa in an adjacent room separated from the TV area by a two-sided fireplace. "Have a seat." Violet picked up the box of receipts and her laptop from a chair next to the fireplace.

He smiled. "Nicer working conditions than the office trailer."

"Warmer, that's for sure." Violet sat down next to him on the couch. She placed the box and laptop on the coffee table in front of them. She took off the lid and flattened out the first few receipts. "These receipts seem incomplete. Missing dates."

A niggling feeling dogged him. What kind of businessman kept his receipts in a shoe box without dates? As outwardly confident as he always tried to portray himself, sitting here in Jacque Caldwell's mansion with his supposedly professional business transactions in a kid's shoe box left him feeling completely out of his element. He shook off the feelings. He wasn't that same cocky young man anymore who had to prove his salt by being a tough guy.

Theo picked up the first receipt and examined it. There was no date and he couldn't read the handwriting. "I'm going to have to consult with Chad on a few of these." He shook his head. "We had really meant to be disciplined about staying organized, but then orders started rolling in. I suppose it's a good problem to have. With the improving economy, more people are spending money on luxuries like play sets."

"I'm glad to hear it. I imagine growing a business is very fulfilling." Violet smiled ruefully.

"Your mother's enterprises are successful. Or so I hear."

"Yes, my mother has some definite ideas on her brand. But she also has the added benefit of fame. No one's going to offer just anyone a clothing line or a perfume."

He could tell he'd touched on a sore spot so he picked up another receipt. He sensed she didn't begrudge her mother her success, but she did seem to wish she had been born into a less public life. "You have software you'd like to show me?"

Violet nodded and pulled her laptop up into her lap.

Sitting close to her, Theo angled his head and studied her. "You seem a little out of sorts."

She ran her finger over the touchpad, then stopped. She sighed heavily. "Truth?"

He jerked his head back in surprise. He hadn't expected her to open up to him. "I generally prefer the truth," he joked, trying to lighten the mood.

Theo followed Violet's gaze over to his son, visible around the brick wall containing the two-sided fireplace. Liam was absolutely transfixed by the TV program. That was why he rarely let his son watch it. He became like a zombie. Never mind that Theo had watched hours and hours of TV when he was a kid, and for a while there Theo wasn't sure if he was ever going to get on the right path. He couldn't blame his father, though. His father did the best that he could as a single dad. And Theo was now doing the same with more resources than his father had.

"Okay, what's going on?" Theo urged.

Violet stood and walked toward the kitchen. Theo followed. She crossed the room to the French doors and shook the handle, as if to convince herself it was still locked.

"What is it?" he asked, placing his hand on the small of her back.

"Earlier when I was working, the French doors—well, the one French door—blew open."

He furrowed his brow at her. He quickly gazed around. "Do you think someone broke in?"

She bit her lower lip but didn't say anything, as if her boldness in telling him had evaporated like water on the roof of a car on a hot day.

She plowed her hand through her dark hair. She looked far different than the confident businesswoman who first appeared in his office yesterday. Maybe he wasn't the only one practiced at putting on a false front.

"I don't know what to think. I mean, yesterday someone shoved four screws in my tire. I have a right to be worried, right?"

"Of course you do." Then he remembered what Chad had said about Abby's murder. Her body being found in Violet's apartment. Running off the road had only been the latest misfortune Violet experienced. "I'll take a quick look around."

"I'd appreciate that."

"Then I want you to tell me what's *really* going on."

~

Violet stared out over the expansive yard stretching down to the lake as Theo checked outside the property. She couldn't remember the last time she had relied on a man. On anyone. She had prided herself on her independence. She had worked hard and overcome much to achieve it.

But it had come at a cost. She didn't know how to reach out to someone when she did need help. It felt too much like weakness. And weakness felt like failure.

Instead, she bottled up her fears and suffered debilitating panic attacks as a result.

Violet stared past her reflection in the French doors and startled when she refocused her gaze on Theo striding across the lawn directly toward her. She pulled open the door.

"Anything?" She hated how her heartbeat sounded loudly in her ears, making the single word sound breathless and scared.

"There are tracks." Large snowflakes dotted his hair. She resisted the urge to reach up and brush them off and instead tucked her arms in a tight fold across her chest, waiting for him to continue. Tell her it was deer or a bunny. Something cute and harmless. "It's almost as if someone was trying to disguise their tracks by dragging a branch across the snow."

Violet ran a hand across her mouth. "Not a deer?"

He gave her a curious gaze. "A really smart deer?"

Violet laughed, a high-pitched nervous sound that pierced her ears. "Where did the tracks lead?"

"Into the tree line."

Violet shook her head slowly, trying to get her head around this.

"You want to tell me what's going on?"

She bit her lower lip and slipped onto a stool at the

kitchen island. In the background, Liam giggled at a cartoon. "Maybe we should talk about this another time."

"Liam's not listening." He slipped onto the chair across from hers and rested his hand on her wrist. The coolness of his touch felt good. "Talk to me. Yesterday someone gave you a flat tire. Today someone's lurking outside. Maybe tried to come in." Theo slid off the chair and glanced toward the sounds of the television. "Any chance someone's in your house?"

The bottom dropped out of Violet's stomach and the floor shifted. "No, not possible. I was sitting by the fire. If someone came in, they would have only gotten as far as the kitchen before I saw them."

"Are you sure?"

"Yes, absolutely. But why make the effort to come that far?"

"You tell me." He dragged the stool closer to hers and sat back down, his knees brushing hers.

She took a deep breath, wondering how much she should share. He had burned her before, but something in his warm brown eyes made her take a chance. "My stalker's back."

Theo's eyes flared wide. "From when you were a teenager?"

Theo had been the only person she had ever confided in from Hunters Ridge High School. She'd told him about her stalker and the panic attacks that had led her to the big house on the hill.

"I…" She immediately began to doubt herself. *Isn't that what my mother always makes me do?* "I mean, it only makes sense."

Instead of leaning back and laughing and telling her she was imagining things, he rested his elbows on his thighs and pulled her hands into his. "What's been going on?"

Violet let out a long, slow breath between tight lips. "It

always starts out as an inkling. Like someone's watching." She shrugged, feeling the intensity of his gaze searching her face. Then he started to smooth the pad of his thumb across the back of her hand, giving her an alternate focal point that calmed her nerves. "But I can't trust myself." She drew in a deep breath before continuing. "When I was twelve, thirteen, I was convinced I had a stalker then, too. Turns out my paranoia resulted in a photographer—paparazzi—getting detained. My mother was livid. Jacque Caldwell is of the 'no publicity is bad publicity' school of thought, unless it's your daughter acting crazy."

"You're not crazy," he said softly.

She tilted her head. She felt crazy.

"That photographer was well respected and often sold photos to top magazines. My mom couldn't deal with me anymore. Shortly after that, she moved me here." She smiled even though sadness pulled at the corners of her mouth. "But you already know all that."

"They never made an arrest back then?-"

She shook her head. "Two months ago, someone broke into my apartment and killed Abby."

"I'm sorry." The sympathy in his eyes was almost her undoing. "Chad told me. He had read about it in the papers. I guess I was out of touch."

"Well, the police dismissed it as her being in the wrong place at the wrong time, but I feared someone had broken into my apartment to get close to me and found Abby instead. Killed her." She struggled to swallow around her dry mouth. She searched his face and he seemed to be waiting for her to continue. "There's no proof. Just a feeling. That same creepy feeling of being watched." She waved her hands in dismissal. "I'm being silly." That's how she had been made to feel.

"Stop dismissing your concerns. Talk to me."

She hiked her chin. "I remember talking to you once. It ended up blowing up in my face." Her gaze drifted to the counter behind him. The butcher block of knives sat tucked in the corner. The fear from earlier, of feeling alone and trapped and wondering if she could use a steak knife for protection sent a fresh wave of apprehension rolling over her. She had to trust someone or she'd go…crazy.

"I never meant to hurt you." His thumb kept up the steady back and forth across the back of her hand.

It was her turn to wait for him to continue. He had tried to talk to her after the prom, but she had been so humiliated and angry, she'd refused his calls. Ignored him the few times she bothered to show up at school, the dwindling days of high school prior to graduation.

"I never told Jenny that you were a pity date."

Her eyes snapped up to meet his. Those were the exact words Jenny had used when she cornered Violet in the girls' bathroom the night of the prom.

He only invited you because he felt sorry for you. You're a pity date.

Nine years later the memory slammed into her with all the emotions from that night, a night that had started out fun and exciting and ended so horribly. Not so much because of the words, but because of what happened next. Jenny had known exactly how to ruin Violet's night, as if someone had told her.

Violet tugged her hands away from his and casually rested an elbow on the island and dragged her other hand through her hair. "That was so long ago. Don't worry about it." She had offered the words casually, but they sounded stiff. Stilted. Insincere.

"We need to discuss it so we can move past it."

"Why? I'm capable of working with you without dredging

up the past." She pushed back a fraction and the legs of the stool made a horrible screech on the tile floor.

Theo reached out and brushed his fingers across her knee. "Stop doing that. I need you to trust me. To confide in me. Tell me what's going on so I can help you."

Squaring her shoulders, she stared at him, feeling like she had been rushing toward this moment since she first stepped foot back in Hunters Ridge. "You told Jenny about my panic attacks, the one secret I didn't want anyone to know. You humiliated me." Violet hated the tears filling her eyes, revealing her weakness.

A hurt look swept across Theo's handsome features. "I never told her. I kept your confidence. I would never. Why…?" He searched her face.

"After Jenny told me I was your pity date, she pushed me in a stall and held the door closed. I freaked out, started crying and banging on the door. I had an all-out panic attack. I made a fool of myself."

He brushed a hand across her forearm. "I didn't tell her."

Violet lowered her gaze. "By the time she let me out, I was beside myself." She shielded her eyes with her hand. "You should have seen the look in her eyes. She was outright giddy." Violet dropped her hand. "By then, the bathroom was filled with girls from my class. How could I ever face them again? Everything I had worked for…" She let out a long, shaky breath. "I'm just glad I could pull myself together to get away, go to college."

"I'm so, so sorry Jenny did that to you. She's insecure. We dated for most of high school and had broken up shortly before you and I decided to go to prom together."

Violet already knew that.

"Jenny stopped at my house the night before prom in tears, begging me to take her back. Take her to prom. That we were meant to go to prom together. I told her I couldn't because I had already promised to take you."

"Yeah, because you were doing the Weavers a favor because they were friends with your dad."

"That may have been how it started, but I was happy to take you. Yeah unfortunately, I did downplay it to Jenny. Told her I was doing a favor. She was being irrational. I had to tell her something." He scrubbed a hand across his face. "I should have known better. I was young. Immature. But I promise you, I didn't betray your trust. I did *not* tell her about your panic attacks and what had brought you to Hunters Ridge."

She studied his eyes. She believed him. Jealous Jenny was cruel. She didn't know locking Violet in the bathroom stall would cause her to panic.

"Apparently I'm not a quick learner." Theo angled his head to catch her eye, a flicker of humor lighting his. He obviously had gone back to Jenny, a relationship that resulted in Liam. "But I think God had a hand in that. I don't know what I'd do without that little guy."

Violet smiled at him, debating if she really could trust him. But what choice did she have? And what harm could he do if he did talk? She wasn't a weak seventeen-year-old. She was a young woman who needed a chance to recover after her best friend was murdered. No shame in that.

Violet cleared her throat. "I don't have any proof, but I'm convinced my stalker killed Abby and is now in Hunters Ridge. I think he's having fun taunting me because heaven knows he's had plenty of opportunity to do far worse."

CHAPTER 8

*V*iolet found the keys for her mother's SUV in a lockbox in the mudroom next to the garage. She palmed the weight of them, debating if she really wanted to take out the oversized vehicle. It would certainly be more solid in the snow, but Violet had never driven anything that large.

After her confession last night, Theo had convinced her to call his sister, Deputy Olivia Cooper, to report the two suspicious incidences. Once faced with the uniform, Violet tried to skirt around her stalker theory—that had been her default after all the years her mother had told her she had been imagining things—but Theo convinced her that law enforcement needed to know every angle.

Violet stuffed her feet into her shoes and stepped down the two stairs in the attached garage. She climbed behind the wheel of the large SUV and pressed the remote clipped to the visor. Through the rear-view mirror she watched as the garage door rumbled as it climbed up the tracks. She found herself automatically searching the snow on the driveway for any suspicious tracks.

Nothing, thank goodness.

Isaac and Betty had arrived home last night while Olivia was still there. They assured her that they'd make sure the house alarm was set and that all the doors and windows were locked. Their presence made Violet feel calmer.

She wasn't alone. And after last night, she now felt Theo was firmly on her side, too.

Violet adjusted all the mirrors on the SUV and wondered when the last time was that someone had driven this beast. It was only a few years old—one of her mother's assistants had probably automatically kept a newish vehicle in the garage, just in case—and had less than a thousand miles on the speedometer.

Violet backed out, careful not to take off the mirror on the side of the garage. *Huge accomplishment!*

The thoughts that kept her awake last night continued to swirl in her head as she drove to work. She wondered where reality stopped and her obsessive thoughts took over.

Last night, Olivia had pressed her regarding any other enemies she might have. She had laughed and told her she hadn't been in Hunters Ridge long enough to make enemies, but she knew that wasn't necessarily true. The Graber family wished their lovely daughter had never met the likes of Violet, and Jenny made no bones about her dislike for her. But were either angry enough to try to hurt her? And did that make sense? Violet had found Abby's body in her apartment in New York before her run-ins with Elmer and Jenny in Hunters Ridge. It made more sense that her stalker had followed her to Hunters Ridge. *If* any of this even made sense at all. How would he have found her here? Her mother's country home had been a well-kept secret except for a few of her fellow high school classmates from years ago. And the New York City police considered Abby's death a case of wrong place, wrong time.

Oh, my head hurts.

When Violet finally pulled into the parking lot at work, a strange realization swept over her. She had been so focused on driving an unfamiliar vehicle—things like, did she have to twist the knob or lift the lever to turn up the wipers? Where's the defrost control? How does the seat move up?— that she had forgotten to obsess over any potential body symptoms that would indicate the beginning of a panic attack. Not to mention that her thoughts had been focused on who was out to get her. She laughed at the irony. Maybe Betty had been right all along. Getting out of the house was the first step to managing her anxiety, and God willing, getting over it.

And back to the life she had left behind.

But first, they had to figure out who was harassing her. A twinge of panic tingled in her fingers.

Stop.

Two steps forward, one step back.

Deep breath.

Violet grabbed the laptop and the box of receipts from the back seat and made her way to the trailer. Tucking the box of receipts under her arm, she turned the door handle and it stuck. She adjusted the strap of her laptop case over her shoulder and tried to open the door again. A rustling sounded behind the door, then it sprung open. Theo stood in the doorway dressed in jeans and a hunter green sweater. The color suited him.

Theo examined the door handle, jiggling it. "I need to fix that. One of these days I'm going to find myself locked inside."

Violet stepped into the trailer and bumped her shoulder against his solid chest. "Sorry." She scooted around him and set her laptop down on the edge of the desk.

"How'd you sleep?" he asked, his voice low.

"I've had better nights, but I'm glad everything is out in the open."

"Me, too." He smiled. The silence stretched into an awkward moment. "So, you brought your own laptop?"

Violet pointed at his desktop. "Your computer is pretty old."

"I guess it's one more thing I need to upgrade with my growing business."

"It's okay. I can use my laptop and software, and before I'm done we can upgrade your systems and I can show you and Chad how to use it."

Theo planted his hand on his hip and looked around. "I should really get another desk in here. Or maybe I can set one of those art desks in the corner. That's what I need to design more play sets."

Violet slid behind the desk and sat. She moved some papers around to study one of his renderings. Beside the sketch of an elaborate play set, he had illustrated a yard and a family in the background. She ran her fingers over the images of the little children and the dog. She looked up and they locked gazes. "You're really good at this."

The color in his face seemed to darken and he ran a hand over his hair in what she interpreted as a nervous gesture. He took a step closer and stared at the sketch over her shoulder. "I thought maybe seeing the big picture would help to sell the play sets."

"We'll have to get a computer with enough memory for design software."

He seemed to be considering this for a moment. "I thought including a hand-drawn sketch as instructions was part of our small town charm. Reflects our 'Made in America' thing going on here. People also like the Amish angle, too. They have a reputation for quality."

Violet nodded slowly. "That's a really great idea. I like it. Keep our options open, right?"

A slow smile crossed Theo's handsome features. "Maybe I'm not so green on this business stuff after all."

Violet leafed through some of the receipts stacked on his desk. "Where did these come from?"

"Chad had them in his truck." He shrugged, as if to say sorry.

"No problem."

Theo's eyes brightened. "You want a tour of the facility? I can show you how we put the kits together."

Violet planted her hands on the desk and pulled herself to a standing position. She tugged on her shirt and brushed a hand across the thighs of her jeans. "Sounds great. These receipts aren't going anywhere."

Theo held the door open to the warehouse for Violet. She stepped over the threshold and her wide brown eyes took everything in. A sense of pride filled him. The room hummed with activity. He was proud of himself for continuing the tradition started by his grandfather, handed down to his father and uncle, and now him.

His cousin Chad was in on this, too, when he bothered to show up. He made a big show of getting more business, but Theo wasn't stupid. He could get the same clients in a fraction of the time. But their grandfather had started the business and the third generation had equal stakes in it.

"How many people do you employ?" Violet asked.

"Twenty-seven. Twenty of whom are Amish." He scanned the room. Men in black broad-brimmed hats worked at various stages of production. Even a few women in bonnets were employed here. This was a drastic change in the Amish community, from farming to industry.

"I often wondered how the Amish felt about their young men and women leaving the farms," Violet said, walking slowly along the first workstation where an Amish man cut boards. She had to take a few steps away and raise her voice to be heard over the power saw. "And the issue with electricity? When I was in high school, I often felt like I lived in a different world. My mom could afford this beautiful home on the ridge, then we'd come into town and see the Amish families with their horses and buggies. It always seemed surreal. Almost like when my mother had some business in Williamsburg, Virginia and her assistant took me to see the reenactors. Except—"

"The Amish are not reenactors."

"Exactly."

"Well, as much as the Amish don't want to change, want to keep everyone on the farm—they feel working the land is how they can be close to God—in this economy, it's not always practical. Land is expensive." With a hand to the small of her back, Theo guided Violet toward a pile of two-by-fours. "I've had the privilege of talking to the bishop. He'd rather see the young men employed here in town, rather than getting into the vans and working construction in cities away from here. It minimizes the influence of the outside world if they don't have to leave Hunters Ridge."

"How do the Amish employees get to work? I've never noticed any buggies outside in the lot."

"We have a van that picks them up in three shifts, their start times staggered by thirty minutes. If they took their buggies, we'd have to house the horses all day. It makes more sense to provide transportation."

Violet nodded while running her hand along a piece of red

cedar stacked on a table ready for the next step on the way to becoming a play set in someone's yard. The fragrant smell of wood wafted up to his nose and it made him nostalgic for a time when he used to come here as a young boy, when it was strictly a lumberyard. He was in awe of the work his father did here. His father was a giant in his eyes. Then, a few years later, Theo's mom abandoned them and he blamed his father. It seemed the logical course because his parents were always yelling. He assumed since his father was louder, it was his fault. The rift between father and son had made his teenage years rebellious.

How wrong he was. His father had stayed.

His mother was never cut out for small town life.

How wrong Theo had been to blame his dad. To act out. To act like a punk who didn't care what anyone thought. It shamed him now. That was why he worked so hard to make sure his father had a retirement where he didn't have to worry about finances or his health.

Theo owed him that much and more for being the one constant force in his life. And Theo was going to be that constant in Liam's life.

Theo shook away the haunting memories and picked up a piece of wood. "This is for our premium kits."

Violet glanced over her shoulder up at him. "Parents are willing to go all-out for their kids."

"You should see the one I built for Liam in our backyard. It has two rock climbing walls, a rope swing and a bridge connecting two elevated playhouses."

Violet lifted an eyebrow and smiled. "You're passionate about this."

"I am." He nodded for emphasis. "When I was a kid, I used to come to the lumberyard and imagine all the things that could be built with the wood. However, it took my dad getting sick for me to come home and take ownership." He scratched his ear, feeling like perhaps he was exposing too much of his soul.

Violet moved toward another workstation where a young Amish woman was making kits of fasteners and other hardware for the play sets and putting them in clear plastic bags. She had on fingerless gloves.

"A little cold in here for you, Lorianne?" Theo asked. Then he looked at Violet who was staring at the young woman—and remembered she was Abby's sister. He kept the conversation casual. "I need to get some estimates on getting this shell of a warehouse insulated."

Lorianne smiled, her smooth white complexion in sharp contrast to her black bonnet. "I don't mind the cold." She lifted her fingerless-gloved hands and waved. "It beats working on the farm in the summer. I don't like to be hot. And farm work is backbreaking. This work"—she lifted a silver hook in her delicate fingers—"is a pleasure. And it helps us get through the winter."

"Hi, Lorianne. How are you?" Violet asked, blotches of pink alighting on her skin.

"Fine." Lorianne suddenly seemed to get shy and dipped her head.

Violet looked like she wanted to say more, but let it drop. She wore the guilt over Abby's death in the delicate lines around her eyes. He wished he knew of a way to lift that burden.

"Nice to see you," Violet said before wandering over to a lower shelf and running her hand along a box. "Kits for the play sets?"

"Yes." He pointed to a wall of boxes on shelving, realizing she probably didn't really care, not as much as she pretended to. Her thoughts were with Lorianne and Abby.

"And all these sets are presold?" she asked, her tone chipper.

He wanted to tell her she didn't need to pretend with him, but decided now was not the time.

"Yes, we've sold them to big box stores. Chad's job. They want them in stock so customers don't have to wait for them. The stores are able to make extra money on these because they charge for installation."

Violet crossed her arms. "Ever think about doing the installation yourselves? Increase the profit margin?"

"We'd have to hire more people. And we'd only be able to install them regionally. Believe it or not, we're selling these kits to stores all across the US."

Violet nodded slowly as if she were deep in thought. "That's great."

"Now you can see why I want to get the finances in order. It's taken off. It's bigger than I ever imagined."

Violet smiled. "I'm happy to help. I can get you organized and either train you or my replacement."

"Already planning for your departure?" A smile teased the corners of his mouth.

"I didn't mean that. I just wanted to reassure you that once I get an accounting system in place, I won't dump it off and run."

"Good to know."

Theo's phone rang and he grabbed it and swiped his hand across the screen. "It's Liam's school," he whispered, a twinge of nerves tangling in his gut. A call from school midmorning generally wasn't a good thing. "Hello."

"Mr. Cooper?"

"Yes."

"This is Principal Elizabeth Finley. I have Liam here in my office."

"What's wrong?" The idea of broken bones, an upset stomach, unfinished homework flashed through his mind.

The principal cleared her throat. "Perhaps it would be best if your son told you what happened."

Theo's ears got hot. *This definitely isn't good.* He held up his finger and whispered to Violet, "I need to take this. Feel free to keep looking around. I'll be back in a few minutes."

Pressing the cell phone to his ear, Theo stepped outside. The cold wind bit at his face, but he wasn't focused on that. He was concentrating on the indecipherable mutterings and sniffling from his son on the other end of the line.

"Hi, Dad," Liam said, his voice low and contrite.

"What's up, buddy?" Theo's pulse thudded in his ears. He wasn't sure why he was having such a visceral reaction to a phone call even before he knew what was going on. But he knew it was unlikely the principal was calling him during the day to tell him his son had done well on a spelling test.

"I didn't mean it." Liam's voice was shaky. "But she made me mad."

"What happened?"

"I used a bad word when Molly broke my pencil."

There was so much to analyze in that one statement. Theo crossed his arms to stay warm. "Molly's a girl in your class?"

Liam didn't answer, but Theo could envision him nodding his head, a lock of brown hair dropping over one eye.

"Why did she break your pencil? Maybe she didn't mean to."

"No, she meant it. She told me if I didn't give her my dinosaur pencil, she was going to snap it in half."

"And when you didn't give it to her, she did what she said she was going to do."

"Yeah." Liam sounded a little more confident, as if he sensed his father understood the indignity of it all.

Theo knew there were two sides to every story, but he'd

82

vowed to always back his son. Listen to his side of the story. His son had never lied in the past. "Liam, listen to me. What Molly did was wrong, but you know it's wrong to use bad language."

"I know," Liam muttered, sounding absolutely miserable.

"Have you ever heard me using the word you used?" Theo couldn't imagine what he must have said to prompt a trip to the principal's office and a phone call home.

"No."

"Where did you learn it?"

"Mom said it when I spilled my milk. She was really, really mad. And I was really, really mad when Molly broke my favorite pencil."

Theo scrubbed a hand across his face. "Even adults and people we love make mistakes. You shouldn't have repeated the word. You knew it was a bad word, right?"

"I figured it was, because Mom was angry. It sounded bad."

Theo paced on the gravel parking lot between two parked cars. "You know better. Next time you get angry, don't use bad language, okay? And if you can't handle a situation, go to an adult." Theo watched a Styrofoam cup blow and twirl on the wind. He turned his back and hunched his shoulders as a chill shot down his spine. It pained his heart that he couldn't protect his son from…from everything. "You know you can always talk to me, right?" Theo's own father was a good guy, but he wasn't much of a talker.

"You weren't there, Dad." Liam sounded so small, yet defiant.

"Your teacher can help when I'm not around. You know that, right?"

"Yeah."

"Okay, we'll talk more when you get home. Let me talk to the principal."

He wondered how many calls of this nature Theo's father had received over the years. He figured this was his payback. Payback for all the years of giving his father grief.

"I'll address this at home, Principal Finley. Liam knows better."

"Liam's a good kid. He's never done this before. I thought perhaps he could write a letter of apology to the little girl."

"I trust you'll handle it appropriately. Thank you for letting me know. I'll address this at home," he repeated.

Theo ended the call and slipped the phone into his pocket. He'd turned to go into the warehouse when he heard a loud crashing sound.

Adrenaline surged through his veins and Theo bolted toward the door.

∼

Violet wandered the length of the warehouse. Theo had a nice operation. Her gaze kept drifting to Lorianne, Abby's sister. The family resemblance was striking. Since Abby's murder, Violet had been feeling sorry for herself, but this young woman had lost her big sister. *She* was the one Violet should have been focused on.

A heavy weight pressed on her lungs. The Graber family had lost Abby long before she was murdered.

To distract herself, Violet decided to walk down the aisle of stacked boxes to read the labels while she waited for Theo's return. His pinched expression as he hustled out the door suggested the call might not be good news. She hoped it wasn't anything serious.

Each tag had a schematic of the play set. She smiled. Theo was not only a smart businessman, but he was an artist. These play sets were beautiful and she could only imagine the joy they'd bring the children who were fortunate enough to have one in their backyard.

The sound of a motor whirred behind her. Half aware, she glanced over her shoulder. The operator of the forklift had on full winter gear, probably because he loaded the trucks on the dock where the cold winter winds whipped in through the open doors.

Violet wandered down to the next tag under a large box. The boxes contained kits, including plastic steering wheels and phones and other items. The rock climbing walls and slides were stored separately. They must have decided selling the play sets as all-out kits was more lucrative than having a store piecemeal the play sets.

She ran her hand over the laminated card. Theo put his heart into these designs. This one had two rock climbing walls and a tire swing. She smiled. Perhaps Theo was a kid at heart.

Suddenly, a rustling sounded overhead. Violet glanced up and a few cardboard boxes tipped precariously out of their slot. Instinctively, she lifted her hands to cover her head. At the same time, she jumped back. Her hip hit the ground hard and the box landed on her legs and exploded open in an avalanche of wood, plastic parts and fasteners.

She glanced around, half expecting, half fearing another box to come crashing down on her head. Had she accidentally bumped something? No, she knew that wasn't possible. She was only reading the tags.

The forklift.

It stopped on the other side of the rack. From her position, she saw legs and expensive-looking sneakers through an open slot visible near the bottom of the rack.

Footsteps sounded on the cement. She expected to see the man dressed in his winter gear offering a profuse apology.

Instead the first person she saw was Lorianne bending over her with a concerned look on her face. "Are you okay?"

"I—I—" Violet touched her head, her midsection, for confirmation that she was okay. She slid out from under the parts spilled over her legs. "Yeah, I think so." Her scalp tingled, mingling with the adrenaline pulsing through her veins.

More sounds of running feet. Violet brushed a lock of hair out of her eyes and looked up to find a very concerned Theo staring down at her.

Theo crouched down next to her. "Are you okay? What happened?"

"Yeah." Her face grew hot as she suddenly felt stupid. Embarrassed. Had she somehow caused this? It wasn't like she had never been in a plant before. She knew to be cautious. Aware of her surroundings.

Violet craned her neck. What had happened to the forklift driver?

"What happened here?" Theo tossed a piece of plastic back toward the shelving unit.

"I'm not sure. I think the guy on the forklift knocked the boxes over from the other side of the shelves." Violet pressed her hand against the smooth, cold cement, but her wrist gave out on her.

Theo cupped her elbow. "You okay to stand?"

Feeling a little silly, she smiled sheepishly. "It would be preferable to the cold floor."

Slipping his solid arm behind her back, he helped her up. A twinge of pain shot through her leg when she put weight on it. "You okay?" he whispered close to her ear.

She nodded.

Theo turned to Lorianne who was standing nearby wringing her hands. "See who was driving the forklift. Maybe he doesn't realize he pushed the boxes over."

Deep in her heart, Violet couldn't believe any of this was accidental.

"Can you walk?" Theo asked.

Violet stepped free of Theo to test her ankle. The initial pain didn't seem to be an indicator of anything serious. She could walk on it just fine. "I'm all right."

A look of uncertainty flickered in Theo's eyes.

A moment later, Lorianne ran back over to them. "The forklift is sitting idle on the other side."

"Who was operating it?"

"No one seems to know. There aren't any orders going out. I asked LuAnn in shipping. As far as she knew, Levi, the usual driver, was on a smoke break. No one should have been using the forklift."

Violet dragged a hand across her hair. "I saw a guy dressed for winter operating it. I couldn't see his face."

Theo wrapped his arm around her and led her to the door. "Let's go sit down."

A shudder racked through her body that had nothing to do with the temperature in the warehouse. Someone had tried to hurt her.

Or worse.

Again.

CHAPTER 9

"Are you sure you're okay?" Theo had his arm hooked around Violet's elbow as they crossed the parking lot to his office trailer. She seemed a little hesitant, but grew steadier with each step. He'd be lying if he didn't admit he feared the liability of having an unsafe work environment, but right now his primary concern was for Violet's well-being. He'd deal with the business—and legal—aspects later.

"I'm fine, really." Violet smiled, but her lips twitched slightly when she put weight on her injured ankle. He sensed that her pride had also taken a hit, but he wasn't sure why. By all accounts, a careless forklift driver had tipped over boxes from the racks.

"I'd feel better if you got checked for a concussion. Any other injuries."

"I didn't hit my head." Her hand went to her right hip. "I landed on my cushy backside." She deflected his concern with humor.

She tried to wiggle free of his grasp, but he was reluctant to let go of her. Not just yet.

Theo guided Violet to the small stoop on the front of the

trailer and after fighting with the sticking door a minute he got her inside. "Here, have a seat on the couch."

Theo didn't let go of her arm until she was seated. He dragged the chair around from the front of the desk and placed it directly across from her. "Tell me what happened?"

Violet slumped back into the couch and closed her eyes briefly, as if catching her breath. "I was admiring your designs on the laminated placards on the racks." She got a distant look in her eyes as if she was remembering a particular detail. "There was a guy on a forklift. I'm guessing he bumped the boxes from the other side and they tipped over. It was an accident." Her voice hitched on the last few words, indicating she wasn't so sure.

"We didn't see anyone, but whoever did it left the forklift right where he hit the boxes. I asked Lorianne to send Levi, the young Amish man who normally drives the forklift, to my office." He let out a long breath. "In light of everything else, I don't like this. Not. At. All."

A thin line creased her forehead and she shook her head, as if she didn't want to consider it. "I don't think he was Amish. He was dressed in winter gear. I couldn't see his face, but nothing about his dress seemed Amish. I noticed he had on expensive sneakers." She rubbed the back of her neck. "That doesn't seem Amish, does it?" She shrugged. "Maybe someone else was filling in for your usual person and got spooked when they knocked the boxes over. Took off."

Theo stood. "You okay in here a minute? I'm going to walk the warehouse. See who's around. Figure out what happened."

"Yeah, I'm fine." She pointed her thumb at the desk. "No reason I can't make some headway through the paperwork." Theo reached out to grab the door handle. Violet must have sensed his hesitation and asked, "Everything okay?"

"What do you mean?"

"You got a phone call before I...before I fell on my backside."

Theo's shoulders sagged and he plowed a hand through his hair, then turned to face her. "It was Liam. Well actually, his principal."

Violet's back straightened. "Is everything okay?"

"Yes, it's me who's going to need some help."

She angled her head, listening.

"He got in trouble for his language at school." Theo shook his head. "I'm afraid the kid's come by it all honestly since I'm his dad."

Violet pushed to her feet and a fleeting grimace flashed across her features.

He raced over to her. "Sit down."

Violet waved him off. "I'm okay." She took a step toward him. "Give yourself more credit. I've only known Liam for a few days—and I've seen you with him. He's a great kid." She touched his forearm. "And you're a great dad."

"Thanks. But I'm afraid he's acting out. His mom deserves a chance to be a mom, but what about Liam? Is it affecting him negatively?" He frowned. "Little guy shouldn't have to deal with grown-up situations. I pray every night that I'm doing right by him. I've done my best to be a good dad. Liam used a few choice words at school that he's never heard come from my mouth, but..." Theo vowed he'd never throw the mother of his son under the bus. "He's gotten the idea that it's okay to speak that way."

"He's a little boy. He'll make mistakes. You'll do right by him."

"I'm trying." A hollowness expanded in the pit of his stomach. Theo had grown up without a mother. And the last thing he wanted to do was keep Liam from his. But didn't Jenny also need to prove she was up to the task? Liam couldn't suffer for her mistakes. He ran a hand across his forehead. Why did life have to be so complicated?

"Do you have to go to school? Don't let me hold you up. *Please*." Violet's question snapped him out of his wandering thoughts.

"He's coming home on the bus at dismissal. I'll have a chat with him then." Theo pulled open the door. "Meanwhile, I'll see who was driving the forklift." He patted her hand that was resting on his forearm. "We can't have accidents like this. Stay here." He smiled. "Stay warm. I'll be right back."

But after everything else, something told him this was no accident.

～

Violet tried to focus on work for most of the day, but she was distracted. She had tweaked her ankle when she fell, but figured nothing a day or two of taking it easy wouldn't cure.

Her life was another story. Everything was spiraling out of control.

She could have been killed today if she hadn't jumped back. Her stomach knotted as an all-out panic attack threatened. She quickly pushed the thoughts from her head. She would not allow the anxiety to take root.

Deep breath.

Violet leaned back in Theo's leather desk chair. The soft glow of her laptop with its backdrop of photos from around the world was familiar, comforting. She had spent countless hours behind the laptop, working from points all around the world. Now, here she sat in an uninsulated trailer with an auto parts calendar on the wall and a TV and game console in the corner. She ran a hand down her hair and twisted it around her finger. Realizing what she was doing, she dropped her hand. Twisting her hair was an old habit from high school.

She had to get better so she could travel again. Live life without this constant knot in her gut. She rolled her shoulders, trying to ease the frustration.

A whisper of dread coiled around her spine and made her shudder. The same thought had been haunting her all day. *What if it wasn't an accident? What if my stalker has really found me?* She wasn't a big believer in coincidences. The flat tire. The tracks around her house. The near miss in the warehouse.

Abby's murder.

She bowed her head and threaded her fingers through her hair as panic bit at her scalp. Had her panic now turned to paranoia? How would some random stalker have gained access to the forklift? She bit her lip. It wasn't as if the warehouse was secure. Anyone could have wandered in and taken the opportunity. As if they were watching.

Stalking.

"Oh man, get a hold of yourself," she muttered, hating that she was about to go out of her skin.

The crunching of gravel under tires followed by a car door slamming caught her attention. A moment later, rustling sounded at the door. Chad, Theo's cousin, stepped into the office and gave her an assessing stare that unnerved her. Or maybe it was merely a reflection of her already frayed nerves.

Chad rapped his knuckles on the corner of the desk. "You okay? I got a call there was a commotion in the warehouse. Something about a near miss with you and some boxes." Tufts of his hair stood at odd angles, as if he'd been jamming his hands through it.

Violet lowered the lid of her laptop and it closed with a

quiet click. "Some inventory fell off the top rack, probably nudged by an inattentive forklift driver. I was standing in the wrong place at the wrong time."

"How long ago did this happen? Where's Theo? Does he know what happened?"

"It happened this morning. I'm fine."

Chad paced back and forth in the small space, then spun around to face her. "Unacceptable." He stopped and studied her. "Are you sure you're okay?" A strange vibe rolled off him, or maybe Violet was just surprised by his concern.

Violet held up her hands. "Yes, fine. I promise."

"I better get out there. Get some answers. We need to make sure we have a safe working environment. OSHA will be all over this."

Just then, Theo came through the door and did a double take when he saw Chad standing there.

"I heard what happened. Came to check on Violet."

Something flashed across Theo's face that Violet couldn't quite identify. "I thought you were in Buffalo all day."

"Finished up early. Did you find the driver of the forklift? Was it Levi?"

"No one seems to know who was driving the forklift. Levi was on a break. Left the keys in the truck." Theo looked like he wanted to say more, but instead his gaze drifted to Violet and stayed there.

Chad sat down on the arm of the couch. "Whoever knocked the boxes probably realized their boneheaded mistake. They're probably afraid of getting fired. He could have killed someone."

"I know." Theo crossed his arms over his chest. Violet felt invisible as they talked about the situation as if she wasn't here.

"I'm grateful Violet wasn't hurt." Chad stood. "And I know

you might not agree with this—either of you—but if we report this, we'll have OSHA on us. The fines..." Chad shook his head. "Maybe we should review our procedures so this doesn't happen again. Make sure the forklift is secure. Keys locked in the office when it's not in use."

Violet stood and held up her hands. "This sounds like something the two of you have to discuss. I'm going to step outside for some fresh air."

"No, no need. I'm headed out. I've had a long day." Chad opened the door. "Glad you're okay, Violet. See you later."

The white shade rattled on the door with Chad's departure.

Violet leaned forward and planted her elbows on the desk. "I'm sorry I caused all this chaos." Then her voice grew quiet. "I know it sounds crazy, but what if a stranger"—it felt better to say stranger, rather than stalker —"was able to sneak into the warehouse?" She lifted her shoulders. "I don't know. It sounds crazy. Like I'm paranoid."

Paranoid. There was that word again. That's how she had been made to feel when she was fourteen. No one believed she had a stalker. It wasn't unusual for people to hound celebrities and their children. No one had crossed the line.

Theo met her gaze, and the seriousness in his eyes wasn't what she had anticipated. She had fully expected—no, hoped —he would have dismissed her claims as ridiculous. A simple industrial accident was far less ominous. "I don't like this at all."

"You think it was intentional?" She swallowed hard.

"Well, at the very least, I'm going to have to analyze our storage system to make sure this never happens again."

Part of her felt like he was just humoring her. She liked him even more for it. She wanted with all her heart to believe that Abby's murder was a tragic case of wrong place, wrong time, and the rest of the incidences here in Hunters Ridge were just bad luck.

Really bad luck.

Violet tapped her laptop, feeling foolish. "Perhaps I better stay behind my computer where I'm unlikely to hurt myself."

Theo took a step closer. "This is *not* your fault."

His words sounded familiar. Everyone had told her the same thing when Abby was killed. Yet, at some point she had to take responsibility for the mess her life was in.

And responsibility for her part in dragging Abby away from the safety of Hunters Ridge.

But how? She couldn't reverse time. Bring Abby back.

Her emotions welled in her gut and she willed them back. Maybe she needed to look for the faith she had lost. Maybe then she'd rediscover the life she was meant to live.

It had worked before.

Voices sounded outside the trailer. She stood and pulled back the blind to look out, mostly so she could hide her face from Theo. A white van idled while the Amish workers climbed in.

"Quitting time already?" Violet asked. "I hadn't realized it was that late." A man climbing in turned around and stared at the trailer.

Elmer Graber. Abby's brother.

She grew dizzy.

He hopped into the back of the van before she had a chance to look at his shoes. Was he wearing expensive sneakers like the forklift driver?

She yanked on the door, but couldn't open it fast enough. She had to check.

"What's wrong?" Theo asked, coming up behind her.

"Elmer Graber's outside."

Theo's eyes flared wide. "He doesn't work here. Are you sure it was him?"

"Yes, yes, I'm sure."

Theo yanked open the door and Violet slipped out past him. A sharp wind slapped her face as the red brake lights went out and the van turned left onto the main road.

CHAPTER 10

*V*iolet drummed her fingers on the thighs of her jeans, anxiously watching the markers on the side of the country road as Theo raced toward the Grabers' house.

"You okay?" he asked.

"Yeah," she whispered. The closer they got, the more her panic ramped up, thus her intense focus on the mile markers. They were a distraction. "We need to find Elmer. I need to check out his sneakers." Had he been behind the forklift accident? Elmer blamed Violet for taking her sister away from the Amish community. The hatred in his eyes pressed heavy on her lungs. She blinked and the image of Abby's vacant eyes stared up at her from the kitchen floor. If Abby had never met Violet, she'd still be alive today. Biting her bottom lip, Violet wiggled in her seat and cleared her throat.

"I should probably call the sheriff's department. Have them meet us there," Theo said calmly.

Violet rubbed her lips together, giving his suggestion some thought. Had she made a huge leap just because she saw Elmer hop into a van shortly after she was almost crushed by the weight of a play set? "Let's just go ourselves."

"You're doubting yourself."

"I don't have any proof. It could be a coincidence." She shifted in her seat to get a better look at Theo. "Has Elmer Graber ever taken that van home before?"

He gave her a quick sideways glance, then returned his gaze to the road. "I wouldn't know. He doesn't work for us, but his sister does. Maybe he caught a ride out of convenience. The driver's not picking up his phone, which is good, I suppose. He has strict instructions not to use his cell phone while driving."

She nodded, but didn't say anything.

Theo reached across and took her hand and squeezed it. "You are not responsible for Abigail Graber's death," he said as if reading her mind. "She wanted a different life. You and your mother provided that for her."

"But if she hadn't left..." Her lungs and throat ached. She turned her focus to the warm touch of his hand and a blanket of calm covered her. "Thanks for..." She stumbled to come up with the right word. "Thanks for listening to me and taking me to the Grabers. I'm not sure what we'll uncover, but if anything, it will give me peace of mind."

"Absolutely." He dragged his thumb across the back of her hand, sending tingles of awareness coursing up her arm that had nothing to do with her anxiety. "If someone's messing around in my warehouse, I want to know about it. And put a stop to it."

Violet let her gaze go blurry as the fields whizzed by. At one point, Theo gave a wide berth to a horse and buggy making its way along the side of the road. When Violet first got her driver's license as a teenager, she used to hold her breath when passing a horse and buggy. She was terrified of having a collision and hurting the beautiful animal.

"Here we are." Theo's announcement startled Violet out of her thoughts. He pulled his hand from hers and turned into the Grabers' rutted driveway.

Violet dragged a hand through her hair and it got caught on a knot. "Why am I bothering the Grabers? Have I become that paranoid little girl again?"

"You aren't paranoid. Let's talk to Elmer. Cross him off the list. Or not."

"I hate this feeling, wondering if I can trust myself."

"I trust you." He stared at her for a long minute, rendering her momentarily speechless. She was so used to her mother's kneejerk reaction of dismissing her that she didn't know how to respond to acceptance. "You ready?" he asked, a quizzical look in his warm brown eyes.

Why can't I find a guy like this in New York?

"Because you're too busy working when you're not driving yourself mad over pretend stalkers," came a voice in her head eerily reminiscent of her mother's.

"Ready as I'll ever be," she muttered as she slid out of the truck, a twinge rippling up her ankle. She quickly forgot about her injury as they got closer to the Grabers' front door. Apparently sensing her unease, Theo reached back and took Violet's hand and squeezed it reassuringly. Her heart was nearly beating out of her chest and his hand provided a lifeline. An anchor.

"You okay?"

"Yeah," she whispered, her knees feeling like jelly.

Theo brushed a soft kiss across her knuckles, taking her mind off her ramping anxiety. She didn't have time to process the kiss before he lifted his hand to knock. Footsteps sounded inside. Lorianne appeared and despite the temperatures, she had bare feet poking from underneath her pale blue dress.

"Mr. Cooper?" Her eyebrows raised in surprise. "Violet."

"Sorry to bother you at home," Theo said. "Violet and I need to talk to your brother."

A male voice hollered from the back of the house. "Who's at the door?"

"It's Mr. Cooper from work."

Mr. Graber appeared in the doorway leading to the kitchen. His unkempt beard hung to the middle of his chest. His eyes had the hollow look of someone who had lost much.

Because of me.

She wondered if he knew who she was. Despite being best friends with his daughter, their relationship didn't allow for Violet to meet Abby's family, other than a quick goodbye between Abby and her younger siblings.

Don't think of that. Not now.

"Can we help you?" His weary gaze drifted from Theo to Violet, who was standing slightly behind him.

"Is Elmer home?" Theo asked.

"He's doing some chores before dinner." He cleared his throat. "What's this about?"

Mrs. Graber appeared, wiping her hands on a dishtowel, her hair neatly pulled back and swept up under her white bonnet. An image of what Abby might have looked like twenty years from now, had she lived, flashed in Violet's mind and pained her heart, making any words impossible.

"Hello, Mrs. Graber. We came to see your son," Theo said.

"Why is *she* here again?" Mrs. Graber's voice was barely audible, but the venom in it was unmistakable.

Mr. Graber turned to his wife, his eyes narrowing. "What is it, Lucy? Who is she?"

She dropped the dishtowel to her side. "This is the woman who took our Abigail."

Any words Violet might have spoken got trapped in the emotions clogging her throat.

"We came to see Elmer," Theo pressed.

"He's in the barn," Lorianne whispered.

"Thank you." Theo turned around and placed a hand on the small of Violet's back. He leaned in and whispered, "Let's go."

She looked up at him, her doubts crowding in on her. She had no right to bother the Grabers, but Theo had taken charge. He slipped his hand into hers, forcing her to continue on this path. They went outside and hustled across the hard-packed earth toward the barn.

The pungent smell assaulted Violet before they reached the barn. Abby had told her she loved working at the big house on the hill because everything was so clean. She shared stories of mucking the stalls and feeding the pigs and hating every minute of it. Elmer used to bully his sisters into doing his chores so he could sneak off, even though he was barely a teenager.

Abby had wanted so much more from life, and Violet was her ticket out of Hunters Ridge.

Violet took shallow breaths, trying to stay calm and not get too big a whiff of the farm. She glanced over her shoulder, hearing voices from the house. It seemed Mr. and Mrs. Graber were debating running out there to stop them. She grabbed Theo's arm. "Maybe we should go."

"Hold on."

They slowed as they entered the barn. It took a minute for her to adjust to the lighting in the barn. A row of pigs ate at the trough.

The stench was strong, and Violet decided right then and there that she'd never eat bacon again.

Elmer stepped out of the shadows with a huge bucket, and a disinterested look on his face. Without acknowledging them, he dumped a bucket of slop into the trough and took a step back. He slammed down the bucket and lifted his eyes to hers. A chill skittered up her spine and the walls of the barn closed in on her. Tiny dots danced in her eyes.

"Elmer Graber?" Theo asked.

"*Yah.*"

"I'm Theo Cooper and this is—"

"I know who that is."

"We noticed you caught a ride in the van from the lumberyard."

Elmer lifted his eyebrow as if to say, *So what?*

"The van is for my employees."

The young Amish man tilted his head. "What? You come to collect the fare?" A harsh laugh escaped his lips. The entire time he spoke, he kept his eyes on her.

Violet squared her shoulders and her mother's advice floated to mind. *Never let them see you sweat, sweetie.*

"That's not it." Theo made a move toward him and Elmer's brow furrowed.

"I caught a ride, that's all. I work at the cheese factory in town. Sometimes I use the van your company provides."

"I have no problem with that."

"What is it, man?" His words carried the slight lilt of Pennsylvania Dutch. Even after spending her high school years here, Violet only knew a handful of words of the Amish language. The fact that the language survived all these years shouldn't have surprised Violet considering how committed the Amish were to staying separate.

Violet touched Theo's arm, wanting a chance to speak before the conversation took a wrong turn. "I saw you and thought maybe you were looking for me." She watched his reaction carefully. "Perhaps you wanted to talk."

"I said all I need to say to you when you came out here the other day. I want nothing to do with you. You ruined my family."

The words "I'm sorry" got lodged in her throat. She had

already apologized and this was not a man looking for an apology.

She took a step to the right, to see his feet. Her heart sank. His shoes were covered in mud from the pigpens. She couldn't tell if they were the same shoes she saw the forklift driver wearing. She glanced at Theo and shook her head slightly.

Elmer glanced down at his feet, his eyes hidden by the brim of his hat.

"We shouldn't have bothered you." Violet turned to leave.

"Hey," Elmer shouted after them. "I take that shuttle home because I need to look after Lorianne. I promised my *mem* and *dat* that I would."

Theo nodded. "Sorry to have bothered you."

Once they were on the road again, Theo turned to Violet. "Do you think it could have been Elmer on the forklift?"

The weight of recent events weighed heavily on her chest. "I don't know. I really don't."

"We'll report the incident to Olivia. We'll find out who did this."

Violet made a sound that suggested she wasn't so sure. "I came back to Hunters Ridge because I thought I'd be safe like I was in high school. What if whoever killed Abby has followed me here?"

"No one knows your mother owns this property, right?"

"No, except for a few of the local residents."

"You know, you never told me why your mom chose Hunters Ridge to begin with," Theo said, no doubt sensing she needed a distraction. "How does a person who splits their time between New York and Los Angeles find a house here? It's pretty remote."

"Once my mother's frustration level with my panic attacks reached her limit, she knew she had to do something with me." She frowned. "I was cramping her style. I refused to get on a plane. I wouldn't leave the apartment. The pediatrician said a lot of kids have panic attacks when they go through puberty." She shrugged. "I was at that age and I was convinced I had a stalker." Violet shook her head. "My mother joked with an assistant that she wished she could find someplace that didn't have paparazzi, where we could get away from it all. Turns out, her assistant used to drive through Hunters Ridge on her way home to Buffalo from New York City and had admired the house. Some bigwig in the cable TV industry had built the home before getting convicted of embezzlement. The house was empty, my mom wanted a getaway and that's how I ended up in here."

"That's pretty random."

"Life seems that way sometimes." She stared at the black snow on the side of the road. Temperatures were going to get warmer and it would melt, but they had a long winter ahead of them. "Initially I felt abandoned because my mother never came here as often as she promised. But Betty Weaver was the best thing that happened to me. She has a way of grounding me." Having said that aloud, Violet realized something that deep down she knew, but had forgotten: Betty lived her life simply. She had left her Amish roots, but continued to dress in clothes that weren't flashy, she didn't acquire stuff, and she seemed to enjoy each moment whether she was cooking or doing cross-stitch. Violet should take a lesson from her.

"Life has a way of working out sometimes." Theo smiled, but kept his eyes on the road. A warmth spread through her heart.

How was her life meant to work out? She wished she knew.

Maybe Violet's goal of getting over her panic so she could jump back into her old life was misguided. Maybe she needed to slow down and enjoy the moment. Her gaze drifted down to Theo's hand entwined with hers. Maybe her old life wasn't where her future stood.

She glanced at the fields passing by. Could she stay here long-term? Wouldn't she get bored? What about her mother? Jacque claimed she needed her daughter working for her. And Violet liked making her mom proud.

CHAPTER 11

For the second night in a row, Violet woke up in the throes of a panic attack—shortness of breath, dizziness, tingling fingers. The walls of her bedroom growing closer. Suffocating. It took a few long, anxious moments for her to recognize where she was. To realize she was safe.

For now.

She had spent all of yesterday curled up by the fireplace with a good book and tea, hoping she'd be able to relax and forget about the mess her life had become. And alternating between thinking her stalker had returned or perhaps Elmer Graber was out for revenge.

Lying flat on the bed, she stared at white lines stretched across the ceiling from the glowing moon. Falling back asleep didn't seem likely. She couldn't turn off her brain.

Yesterday, she had placed a call to the detective in charge of Abby's murder case in New York City. No arrests, but they had picked up a guy last week out on the fire escape of a neighboring building. They speculated that the murderer had gained entry to her apartment through the fire escape.

However, last week's guy was a Peeping Tom. Nothing more. The detective said there was no link, but the implication was simply that crime happens in a big city.

There was still no proof Violet had been the target. The only way they'd get that was when—*if*—they ever arrested someone.

Sweat pooled under her arms so Violet kicked off the covers as the walls heaved and groaned, threatening to close in on her. The air cooled her sweat-slicked skin, bringing her back to the moment.

She feared her life was never going to be bigger than sleepy little Hunters Ridge. Her mother had warned her not to be one of those people afraid to live their lives. Jacque Caldwell came from nothing and became *something*. Violet had been reminded her whole life that she had it so much easier than Jacque had it growing up and she was now squandering her birthright because of silly fear.

Silly fear.

No one who suffered from panic attacks would ever call them silly. Violet knew her symptoms were a creation of her overactive imagination. That her fears were mostly irrational. But anxiety was not a logical master.

Could she ever be content—happy—if her world had truly shrunk down to the thirty-three square miles that comprised Hunters Ridge and its immediate surroundings?

Her mind drifted to the bottle in her coat pocket, then quickly dismissed it. She wanted to do this on her own.

An empty feeling expanded inside her and she rolled over and stuffed her hand under her pillow to plump it, and stared at the shade covering the window. A corner was bent, allowing moonlight in.

What am I going to do? Even forcing herself to do things that triggered her panic had yet to make her immune to it. So much for the cognitive behavior therapy that had worked for her during high school. Now, her battle with anxiety felt like two steps forward, three steps back. Instead of getting better, she was getting worse. She buried her face in the pillow and tried to ignore the knot in her stomach.

Violet had never felt so desperate in her whole life. She had always prided herself on being a smart, independent woman. Yet now, the most content she felt was when she was home with Betty or—if she were being honest with herself— when Theo was by her side.

Heaven help me.

At some point, Violet had drifted back off to sleep, and now she woke up to the mechanized rumble of the automatic garage door opener. Isaac and Betty must be headed off to church. Betty had to go in a little early to help set up for a breakfast that was going to be held after the service. In her despair last night, Violet had told Betty not to wake her. A ping of guilt nudged her as she stretched across and picked up her phone, surprised to see it was after nine a.m. The least she could have done was humor Betty and help at church, considering everything she had done for her.

Violet swung her legs over the edge of the bed and pulled on the roller shade until it snapped up with a loud clack. The snow was coming down heavily. Tracks from Isaac's truck lined the driveway.

She thought of Betty's words when they chatted yesterday: *Rely on faith.*

Violet closed her eyes and drew in a deep breath. The thought of getting behind the wheel of the SUV and driving on the snow-covered roads threatened to extinguish her flickering hope. She couldn't push herself today. She felt like she was in a huge gerbil wheel, running, running, running, but unable to escape her rioting emotions.

Rely on faith.

A burst of courage made her grab her phone from the bed where she had tossed it. She scrolled through her recent calls and dialed Theo's number before she lost her nerve.

He answered on the second ring. "Morning, Violet."

He sounded downright cheery.

"Morning." She found herself smiling. "Are you a morning person?" She blinked away the gritty feel of her eyes from her restless night of sleep.

"Is that why you called? To check my mood this morning?"

She laughed. Theo had a wonderful sense of humor. She remembered him as the class clown in high school. Back then it seemed obnoxious. She was too young to realize it was a way of coping. Eventually they had become friendly, but it took looking past his rough edges. Then Jenny saw to it that they didn't remain friends.

"I was wondering if you were going to church this morning."

"Daddy!" Liam shouted in the background.

"Hold on," Theo said to her, then to his son, "Go brush your teeth."

"Oh, I'll let you go," Violet said, suddenly losing her nerve. She wasn't used to asking people for favors.

"No, I have a little more time. Yes, Liam and I are headed to church this morning. He needs a little encouragement to move quickly otherwise we'll be late." His voice sounded husky. "Did you need something?"

"This is going to sound silly, but I was wondering if you could pick me up. For church," she added, as if her request needed clarification.

"Sure," he said. "Service starts at ten."

She suddenly felt like she was outside herself, listening to herself ramble. "I'm not too keen on driving, especially in bad weather." A silence stretched over the line. "I shouldn't have asked. It's an imposition."

"No, no. Not at all. I'd be happy to pick you up. I'll be at your house twenty minutes before. Can you be ready?"

Violet opened her closet, scanning the racks of clothes. "Yes."

"Violet?"

"Yeah?"

"I'm glad you called."

"Me, too." She ended the call and stared at the phone, feeling a mix of uneasiness, excitement and hope.

~

Theo watched as Violet's eyes grew as wide as the huge saucer under the large coffee mug spinning slowly over the "Breakfast" sign at a diner in the next town over.

"Do they serve coffee here?" she asked, laughing.

"Yeah! And hot chocolate with whipped cream!" Liam chimed in.

"And hot chocolate," Theo repeated and winked at Violet.

"I've never been here. I usually go to the Hunters Ridge Diner," Violet said. She had been quiet after church, other than to agree to Liam's persistent please, please, *please* take him to his favorite after-church breakfast spot. Actually, it was their second breakfast. They'd stopped briefly to chat with Betty and Isaac and have a donut at the church, but Liam liked his hot chocolate and strawberry pancakes every week from the diner with the big mug on the roof.

"Hunters Ridge Diner is great, but Liam likes this place and the short drive out into the country."

Violet smiled, apparently getting the irony. A kid who lived in the country enjoyed a ride out in the country.

Theo opened the diner door. Liam slipped inside and ran ahead to the hostess stand. Theo could hear him saying, "Three. My new friend Miss Violet came to church with us. Now she's coming to breakfast with us."

The young hostess smiled at Liam and grabbed two over-sized plastic menus as well as a paper kids' menu. Then she turned her smile on Theo and Violet. Violet was a beautiful woman. And polished. Much too polished to be with a rough-around-the-edges guy like him.

He felt a sense of pride as he held a hand to the small of her back as the three of them followed the hostess to a curved bench in the corner of the diner. Violet slid in, while he and his son scooted in on either side of her.

Liam picked up the green crayon and started coloring the leaves on the tree on the kids' menu-slash-placemat.

"Are you having the usual?" Theo asked Liam.

"Yep. Pancakes with strawberries and whip cream." Liam shifted in his seat to face Violet. "The pancakes are really good."

Violet folded her hands and smiled. "Then looks like I'll be having the pancakes…and coffee."

Liam crumbled his face. "I don't like coffee."

Violet scrunched up her forehead and made a confused face, but a light lit her eyes. "How do you know you don't like coffee? Have you had any?"

The little boy shook his head emphatically. "No way. I don't like the way it smells. I know I wouldn't like how it tastes."

"Fair enough." She cut her gaze over to Theo, obviously enjoying herself. Sitting this close, he noticed a hint of yellow in her brown eyes. "Are you a pancake man?"

"Of course." He unrolled his silverware from the paper

napkin and placed it on the table. "Nothing like a couple pancakes to top off the donut I already ate." Theo patted his stomach. Her eyes drifted to his midsection and back up again. Pink blossomed in her cheeks.

The waitress took their order. The three of them made small talk while they waited for their food. Theo was struck by how good this felt. Like a small family. Jenny and he had fallen apart before Liam was even born. They'd never even had a chance.

After Liam was born, Theo mistakenly believed his only responsibility was financial.

Hanging out with Violet and Liam felt easy, comfortable. Right.

Theo scooted a fraction away from Violet and draped his arm over the empty bench next to him. She was just a friend —an employee—who had reached out to him to go to church.

That's all.

Besides, she had no plans to stay in Hunters Ridge long-term. He couldn't break Liam's heart.

He couldn't break his own.

Liam twisted around and knelt on the bench and chatted with a little boy in the booth behind theirs. Someone from his kindergarten class, apparently. This gave Theo the opportunity to talk to Violet uninterrupted.

"I'm glad you came with us this morning." He peeled back the lid on a creamer and dumped it into his coffee. The metal spoon clacked against the white ceramic mug as he stirred.

Violet glanced down, playing with the edges of the napkin on her lap. Then she looked up, her eyes bright. "Me, too. It's been a long time. It was a nice service."

"Did you grow up going to church?"

"No, my mother's not much of a churchgoer, but Betty is." She took a sip of her coffee and a small smile played on her lips. "This is really good coffee. They've definitely earned the big coffee mug on the roof."

Theo laughed. "Ah, yes."

"You know..." Violet tipped her head. "I felt at peace at church this morning. More at peace than I've felt in a long time."

"I'm glad." Theo covered her hand with his.

Liam was in a long discussion with his friend about whether or not they might have a snow day tomorrow if it kept snowing. He didn't want to squash the boys' enthusiasm by reminding them that it had to snow *a lot* for Hunters Ridge to cancel school. The communities in and around Western New York were experts at efficient snow removal.

"Ah, to be a kid." Violet smiled and pulled her hand out from under Theo's and placed it in her lap. Something flickered in the depths of her eyes that he couldn't quite name.

"Theo!" A loud voice hollered across the diner. He snapped his attention toward the shrill voice and an uneasiness settled in his gut. Liam's mother stormed across the diner, rage heating her face. She jabbed her finger at Violet, and Theo shifted his body to block her, fearing what she might do.

Liam spun around and plopped down in his seat, his enthusiasm draining from his sweet face.

Theo slid out of the booth and stood in front of Jenny, gently touching her arm, but his anger raged hot. How dare she? He whispered, "Not in front of your son."

"That's right." Jenny lowered her voice a fraction and glanced around, as if suddenly aware that people were watching her. "He's *my* son."

"Don't do this," he whispered.

Jenny's eyes flashed angry at Violet. Obviously ignoring him, she plowed forward. "I came here because I thought we could have a family breakfast like we did a few weeks ago."

Theo should have known better than to invite Jenny to breakfast at the time, but it seemed like the civil thing to do. Now it was blowing up in his face.

In Liam's.

"Stop, Jenny. Don't do this in front of Liam." Theo glanced over his shoulder, and his son was sitting in the booth staring up at his parents with wide eyes as if he had done something wrong. Violet had her arm around him in a comforting gesture.

Sadly, this wasn't unlike his own childhood. His mother who was always angry until she finally left his father and her family. He often wondered if she ever found happiness.

Jenny's expression softened a fraction, but the anger still burned bright in her eyes. She leaned over and gave Liam a perfunctory peck on the cheek. "Everything's okay."

"Hi, Mommy," he said, and the eagerness in his tone broke Theo's heart.

"Would you like to join us?" Violet patted Liam's shoulder, then pulled her arm out from around him.

The question caught both him and Jenny—based on her expression—off guard.

"I'm not very hungry any more." She leaned over and tweaked Liam's nose. "I'll see you in a few days, okay little man?"

"Okay, Mommy."

Jenny nodded at Theo, then Violet, a wary look in her eyes. She strode over to the counter and ordered a coffee to go.

Liam got back up on his knees and asked his buddy in the booth next to theirs for a red crayon. He didn't seem any worse for the wear. But he was. Every incident like this had a way of wearing down a kid.

Theo sighed heavily and turned to Violet. "Thank you.

You didn't have to invite her to eat with us." He kept his voice low.

"She's his mom." Violet shrugged. "I don't understand her anger, but I imagine she must love Liam dearly."

Emotion clogged his throat. Theo's gaze drifted to Jenny and he wondered how he could have been attracted to someone like her, and then, now someone like Violet. Two very, very different women.

Perhaps when he connected with Jenny, he hadn't thought he was worthy of someone like Violet. Not that Jenny wasn't worthy of love and happiness, it's just that she had turned to drugs to seek it. She hadn't found herself worthy of love either.

Liam plopped down in his seat when the waitress approached with their food. His son's entire face lit up as he licked a dollop of whipped cream from his fork. He seemed unscathed by the scene played out by his mother. Theo wasn't sure that was a good thing. Maybe Liam had grown accustomed to her behavior, and this was not acceptable.

Theo tracked Jenny until she walked out the door.

"Those look like they're really good." Theo's focus shifted back to his son's plate. Violet wiped a blob of whipped cream from his son's cheek with a napkin.

His heart constricted.

No matter the twists and turns in the road, Theo was forever thankful that God blessed him with his beautiful little boy.

And perhaps Violet Jackson had entered their lives for a reason. A reason far more important than organizing his financial records.

CHAPTER 12

By midweek, Violet was making progress, getting through a lot of receipts uninterrupted and setting up new record-keeping software. Theo hadn't had much time in the last few days. She had hoped he could sit down with her so she could show him the software. It wouldn't be too hard to train someone, *if* they had the time.

And that's why they had hired her. Neither of the men seemed to have much idle time to sit and do paperwork.

Violet leaned back in the chair and crossed her arms. Light flurries swirled in the gusty winds visible through the slats of the blinds. The space heater seemed to be working better today, keeping her toes warm and making the trailer seem a little stuffier than usual, so Violet lit a vanilla candle she had brought with her. She never liked the smell of burnt lint on a heater.

She ran her finger across the mouse pad and her screen came to life. She got back to work and she wasn't sure how much time passed when she heard a jiggling at the door handle. A spike of adrenaline surged through her veins and her palms went slick. The events of last week still had her on edge.

Rolling her eyes, she scooted out of her chair, realizing she was being absolutely ridiculous. She pulled back the thin roller shade and let out an awkward, sharp laugh. "Liam!" Violet released a sigh. The mind was a powerful thing. She turned the handle and tugged on the door until she finally pried it open. Theo really needed to fix that sticking door.

Liam stepped into the trailer with his bright blue winter coat, matching knit hat and gloves. His backpack nearly dwarfed him. "Hi, Miss Violet."

"Hi, Liam. How was school? I thought you were staying after today." Theo had run an errand and had told her that Liam had planned to stay after school for intramural sports.

"I changed my mind. They were going to play badminton." He spit out the last word as if it tasted bad.

"Not a fan of badminton?"

"Nope. Last time I played, I broke a racket and got in trouble."

Liam dropped his backpack and shrugged out of his coat and tossed it on the couch.

"Do you have a lot of homework?"

"Done. It was easy. I did it on the bus."

Violet picked up his backpack and groaned. "What's in here? Rocks?"

"Library books. We can take as many as five out of the library."

"And let me guess. You took five?"

Liam plopped down on the couch and leaned over the backpack and unzipped it. He pulled out a thick textbook-type book, *1001 Practical Jokes*, and handed it to her. She flipped to a random page. "Oh, you better not short-sheet your dad's bed. He might get cold."

"He'd laugh. My dad can be silly sometimes."

Violet closed the book. "He probably would laugh." She imagined the smile lines around his warm brown eyes. "What other books did you pick out?"

Liam's eyes lit up. He reached into his backpack and pulled out an action adventure book that looked more like a middle school reader.

"Can you read this book? It has a lot of words." She fanned through the pages, and breathed in the smell of library books and smiled. She had spent hours upon hours in the Hunters Ridge library with Betty. She loved to read.

"I can read a few words." Liam took the book out of her hands. He opened to the first page and ran his finger down the words, reciting the familiar ones. "The…and…can…"

Violet pressed her hand to her heart. The little boy reminded her of herself. She'd wanted so desperately to be able to read books that were several grade levels above her own. She had a lot of time to practice in her mother's Manhattan apartment where she was often left to her own devices, sitting at the well-heeled feet of her mother's assistants.

"Would you like me to read it to you?"

Liam looked up, eagerness lighting his eyes. "Do you have time?"

Violet glanced over at her desk, the pile of work waiting for her. He was obviously a little boy used to asking the adults in his life if they had time, especially when he got off the school bus and came to his dad's place of work.

Shouldn't little boys be going home to warm homes, mothers' kisses and chocolate chip cookies? She smiled at the silly notion. It wasn't the fifties where mother wore pearls and had time for baking. She bit her lower lip and looked around. But was coming "home" to this work trailer the proper place for a five-year-old boy? It wasn't her place to decide. But for now, she'd give him the attention he craved.

"Of course I have time." She slipped in next to him on the comfy couch and opened the book. "You ready?"

Liam nodded and leaned into her, resting his head on her arm. An emotion she couldn't quite define settled in her chest and made it hard to breathe.

She opened to the first page and started to read. Near the end of the first chapter, Liam's head bobbed forward. Violet angled her head to see his face. His eyes were closed, his long lashes sweeping across his sweet cheeks. A lock of hair swept down on his forehead.

She maneuvered him and placed his head on a pillow. She stared at him for a long minute before standing up. She planted a kiss on his forehead. He smelled like snow and cold, little boy sweat and kid shampoo with a hint of vanilla from the candle.

She glanced toward the door and shuddered at the heavy snow now blowing across the parking lot, covering the cars in a thick layer of snow. A tingling of panic squeezed her heart. She'd have to drive home in this.

Her gaze fell back to the little boy on the couch, peacefully asleep. He still had a few hours before his father could take him home. She remembered seeing homemade cookies in the break room inside the main warehouse.

Violet covered Liam with the blanket draped over the back of the couch, deciding she'd go across to the warehouse and get some hot chocolate for Theo's little boy when he woke up. Unfortunately, she'd have to leave the cozy warm trailer.

As quietly as she could, Violet tugged on her boots and stuffed her arms into her thick coat. She leaned over the back of the couch to check on Liam. He hadn't moved from when she tucked a pillow under his head and placed the blanket over his little body.

Ah, to sleep the sleep of a child.

Violet tiptoed to the door and turned the handle. A high-pitched screech ruined her plans for a stealth exit. She glanced over, but couldn't see Liam over the back of the couch. She held her breath, waiting for a sound to indicate he was awake. Nothing. Kindergarten seemed to be taking it out of the little man.

She stared in his direction, convinced she'd slip out and get back before he woke up. Even if he did, a five-year-old could manage for a few minutes on his own, right? A niggle of doubt punched her gut.

No, he'll be fine. She'd be gone for five minutes.

Flipping up her hood, Violet anticipated the shock from the cold. She slipped outside and ran across the parking lot. The hood blocked out the howling wind. Amazing how much easier she could manage the winter in the right shoes and coat. She'd have to remember to buy some insulated gloves the next time she was out shopping. She smiled to herself. Was she really thinking about staying in Hunters Ridge longer than she needed to?

Once she learned to manage her panic, did she really plan to stay in small-town Hunters Ridge with its nine-month winters? Her mind drifted to the little boy snuggled on the couch and a warmth coiled around her heart despite the wind whipping at her ears. She thought of Theo, too. There was no denying the attraction there, even if neither of them had acted upon it.

Maybe God did have more than one plan for her. Maybe her life as a world traveler was over, and now His plan for her was something different. She reached the warehouse and yanked open the door. The whirr of a power saw spun in her ears and the smell of the dust reached her nose.

Was this supposed to be part of her new life? Keeping books for a small business? Getting an afternoon snack for Theo's son? Being a part of his life? Their life?

A flash of heat made her yank down her hood and unbutton her coat. An Amish man looked up and tipped his hat in her direction. She smiled and strode across the warehouse to the break room.

Lorianne was wiping down the counters. The young Amish woman turned around and smiled shyly and dipped her bonneted head as if trying not to be intrusive.

"How are you, Lorianne?" Violet wanted to say more, so much more, but she couldn't find the words.

"Fine," She looked up. "Can I get you something?"

"Oh, I can get it. I thought maybe Liam might enjoy some hot chocolate and cookies."

Lorianne grabbed a cup. She shook the packet before tearing off the top.

"You don't have to do that. I can get it."

"Oh, it's my job to do odds and ends around here. Sometimes there's not enough to do."

"You must be a good worker."

Lorianne blushed.

"Abby was a wonderful worker, too. She was an assistant to my mother and she had a skillful way of getting things done even before my mother realized she'd need something done." Lorianne's face grew red and Violet realized she had said too much. Perhaps mentioning Abby had been a bad idea. "I'm sorry. I didn't mean to upset you."

"It's okay. It would be interesting to know what my sister's life was like, but I imagine I shouldn't wonder about that. My parents wouldn't like that."

Violet reached out and took the cup from Lorianne and filled it with cold water. "If you ever want to talk about your sister, I'm here."

Lorianne smiled tightly and pointed to the microwave without saying a word. Violet put the cup in the microwave and turned it on.

"Was Abby good at math?"

"Yes, she was." Violet refrained from explaining some of the jobs Abby had been in charge of, not sure how much she should say.

"I'm good at math, too. I like to do numbers, but the Amish only let us go to school through eighth grade."

"Abby had gotten her high school equivalency. She talked of college."

"Oh." There was a hint of shame to that single word. Abby had been chasing worldly dreams.

An idea came to Violet as if floating down on a flurry of snowflakes. "How would you feel about using math at work? Would that be allowed?"

Lorianne's face grew hopeful. "I guess."

"What about computers?"

The young Amish woman pressed her fingerless gloves to her cape. "Me? I don't know how to use a computer, but I learn quick. The bishop understands the need to use technology in the workplace if it's absolutely necessary."

Violet felt a smile curve her lips. "Would you like me to ask Theo if you could learn how to keep the financial records up to date? It would involve working with numbers and using a computer."

"I would." Lorianne tipped her head shyly, an eager gleam in her eyes. "I do try to keep busy, but sometimes I run out of work to do. I like having a job."

"I'll talk to Theo and Chad. See what they think. The ultimate decision is up to them. They hired me to work for them."

"Okay, *denki*." *Thank you.* "I'd like that. At least I think I would."

Violet pointed at the tray of cookies sitting on the counter. "Do you mind if I bring some of your cookies to Liam? He's in the trailer."

"*Yah.* Please do."

Violet fixed a plate while Lorianne got the cup of hot chocolate out of the microwave.

"Any chance there's still coffee around?" Violet scanned the counter and noticed the glass pot was upside down drying on the rack.

"I could make some instant. Would that be okay?"

"It's fine. But I'll make it."

Lorianne showed her where everything was and they put the water in the microwave. Not exactly the coffee she had grown accustomed to in fancy coffee shops throughout the world, but it would do.

Well, on a cold day it actually sounded wonderful.

Violet wrapped the cookies carefully in a napkin and balanced them on the lid of Liam's hot chocolate. She turned to leave and Lorianne called after her. "How much longer will you be in Hunters Ridge?"

"I'm taking one day at a time." Violet's pulse beat in her throat. She forced a smile and lifted the cups, careful not to knock over Liam's cookies. "Thank you. Liam will enjoy this."

Violet strode across the warehouse, balancing the treats. She turned her back to push open the door, then spun around to face a cold winter slap. She squinted against the snow, unable to lift her hood with her occupied hands.

A whiff of something reached her nose. Her gaze drifted to the trailer. A plume of black smoke poured from the vent in the top of the trailer.

Violet dropped the cups and they landed with a splat at her feet. She broke into a sprint to the trailer, screaming. "Liam! Liam! Liam!"

With her heart racing in her throat, she stomped up the metal stoop. She turned the handle and the door wouldn't budge.

The door!

Panic narrowed her vision. With two hands she twisted the handle and pushed, but the door wouldn't open. Liam was trapped.

Dear Lord, help me!

"Liam! Liam!"

CHAPTER 13

heo climbed out of his truck and immediately heard shouting and banging. Terror seized his heart when he saw Violet pounding on the door of his trailer and calling his son's name. Flames shot out of the window and black smoke pumped into the cold winter sky.

Theo raced across the parking lot. Violet looked up at him with panic in her eyes. "Liam's in there. The door's stuck!" The words came out in breathless gasps. His worst fears were realized.

"Move!" He was barely able to get the single word out through a throat clogged with emotion. When she didn't move fast enough, he grabbed her by the waist and set her aside. Her sobbing ripped through him.

He went into military mode. He had handled far worse situations when he was on duty in the army, but none had tore through his chest and made him think he was going to pass out.

His son was in danger.

His son.

Theo elbowed the glass above the door handle. It shattered, the sound like an explosion with the crackling flames. He feared what giving the fire more oxygen could do, but he had to get his son out. He reached in, scraping his wrist against the jagged glass, and turned the hot doorknob. With a firm slam of his hip against the frame, the door swung inward then jammed against something. Covering his mouth with the collar of his coat, he wedged himself through the partial opening. Nothing would stop him from reaching his son.

"On the couch! He's on the couch," Violet shouted from behind him.

But Theo didn't have to go as far as the couch. His son lay on the floor near the door. Theo crouched down and scooped up his son's limp body. "I gotcha, buddy. I gotcha."

Theo spun around and emerged outside. He gulped in breaths of frigid air, filling his lungs.

"Liam! Liam!" He jostled his son, praying he'd look up at him, as he made his way down the stoop. Violet stood with her hands covering her mouth, the horror in her eyes mirroring that in his soul. A crowd of gawkers had gathered to watch the tragedy unfold.

"Put him down here." Violet held out her arms and pushed back the crowd. She peeled off her coat and laid it on the icy gravel.

Theo knelt down and placed his son on top of it. As he checked his son's airway, he was vaguely aware of Violet telling him she had called 9-1-1.

A flutter of Liam's breath brushed across Theo's cheek. A rush of relief washed over him.

Thank you, Lord.

Liam's pulse seemed steady.

"Liam, it's Daddy. Are you okay?"

Liam coughed and sputtered and struggled to sit up.

"Rest easy. Rest easy." Theo put his hand on his son's shoulder. "Lie back."

Violet got down on her knees and kissed the crown of his son's head. She brushed his hair from his forehead marred with soot. "Liam, I'm so sorry. I shouldn't have left you."

"You were supposed to stay after school for intramurals. Why were you here? Why were you alone?" Theo's absolute fear had morphed into confusion and anger. He could have lost his son.

Violet opened her mouth to answer, tears creating tracks down the smudges on her cheeks. "I went to get him a snack. When I came back..."

Theo's urge to lash out at her for leaving his son alone was quelled when he heard sirens approaching. He waved frantically, redirecting his frustration toward the crowd gathered like seagulls over a child's unattended plate of french fries. "Step back. Step back. Leave room for the ambulance."

∾

"Step back!" The terror and anger in Theo's eyes cut Violet to the core. She pushed off the ground, the gravel digging into the palms of her cold hands. She stumbled back into someone's solid hands.

"It's okay. Everything's going to be okay." It was Lorianne. She must have heard the commotion and come running like the rest of the employees. The sea of black hats and chattering in Pennsylvania Dutch scraped across Violet's already frayed nerves.

"Back up," Violet said as the lights from the siren flashed at the entrance of the parking lot. "Liam needs the ambulance..." Her voice broke over the last word and she saw her tear mirrored in Lorianne's eyes.

She moved forward and held her arms out, creating a path through the crowd for the ambulance. The lights cut across her line of vision. Someone else, someone more commanding, pushed the crowd toward the warehouse to make room for the fire truck.

Violet backed up and found herself at Lorianne's side again. "I shouldn't have ever left Liam."

This was her fault.

A thick band of regret, guilt and terror bound her lungs, making it impossible to draw a decent breath. The black smoke choked her. She concentrated on the firefighters scrambling to do their job, refusing to give in to her panic. Refusing to pass out and deflect attention away from Liam. She felt like she was having an out of body experience, hovering over the chaos, over little Liam. His blue tennis shoes, one untied, as the EMTs lifted him onto the stretcher. Thank God he was alert and leaning toward his father, trying to tell him something. Violet bent over and braced her hands on her knees, trying to catch her breath.

"Are you okay?" Lorianne asked, the subtle lilt of her voice a soothing balm to her fiery nerves.

Violet glanced up at Lorianne and could only see Abby.

Her dear, sweet friend Abby's lifeless body. A crimson trail of blood flowing from her ear—a delicate silver hoop earring pierced her lobe—and disappearing under the collar of her silk blouse. In her memory, Violet's gaze drifted down her friend's arm. Her perfectly manicured fingers were still wrapped around her cell phone with its bedazzled case, something Abby carried around as a joke after a lifetime of being told she couldn't have anything fancy.

"Who would expect a business professional to carry a bedazzled case?" she'd say, then laugh, tossing her blonde-streaked hair over her shoulder. But Violet knew it was more than a joke. Abby wanted to always remember to not take herself too seriously, to remember to see the joy in each moment even with the stress of working for Violet's demanding mother.

The little details of Abby's murder were what kept Violet up at night.

The siren on the ambulance wailed, snapping Violet out of her violent memory and into her current nightmare. *How much time has passed?* The crowd pushed back and the vehicle bobbled over the ruts in the gravel parking lot until it reached the road. The tires spun before gaining purchase and racing toward the hospital.

Violet gasped, and quickly covered her mouth.

"Easy there." A deep voice rumbled behind her, snapping her out of the dark tunnel she was falling down. *Chad.*

"She's fine," Lorianne said, speaking up for her.

"It's okay," Violet said. She didn't need someone to speak for her. "Go on back inside, Lorianne. It's cold out here. And you're getting wet from the overspray." She turned her unfocused gaze to the hose pouring water over the trailer fire.

Quickly turning away, Lorianne disappeared into the crowd in the direction of the warehouse. Guilt cut through Violet. She shouldn't have been so quick to dismiss the young woman. Lorianne was only trying to comfort her.

Violet straightened and turned to face Chad, pushing back the mix of confusion and dizziness. Theo's cousin and business partner gave her a half smile meant to be reassuring, but it only made her feel worse.

"Looks like they got the fire under control. Don't worry," Chad said.

"I'm not worried about the trailer," she bit out, holding the collar of her sweater closed around her neck. "I don't know what I'll do if Liam isn't okay."

"What was the little guy doing in there anyway?" Chad

said, his mouth pursed tight. "Hasn't he been staying after school?"

"Change of plans," Violet muttered.

Chad ran a hand across his forehead and exhaled sharply. "He's gonna be okay." He seemed to be trying to convince himself.

"He was conscious when they took him in the ambulance," she said, trying to reassure him.

"That's good, right? Oh man, I'd hate for anything to happen to my little buddy."

She nodded, and a fresh wave of grief washed over her in a full-body tremble. The cold reality of the situation coiled tight in the pit of her stomach. "I should have never left him alone."

Chad rubbed his hands up and down her arms to warm her up. "Why was he in the trailer alone?" The tone of the question lacked the accusation that she expected.

Violet cleared her throat. "He fell asleep on the couch, so I thought it would be okay if I ran over to the break room in the warehouse to get him a snack." She covered her mouth. "I don't understand…" A pounding began behind her eyes as the acrid smell of smoke filled the air.

"Let's get you inside the warehouse before you freeze to death out here." Chad led her gently by the elbow to the warehouse past the fire truck. Once they reached the break room Lorianne offered them coffee. Violet wrapped her hands around the Styrofoam cup. She doubted she'd ever be able to get warm again.

Chad leaned across the table. "Any idea what happened?"

Violet rubbed her temple, and then the stark reality hit her and she sat upright. "I had lit a candle. It was so stuffy in the trailer." Pinpricks of panic blanketed her skin like a wool blanket wound tight around a newborn. "How could I have been so stupid?"

Chad's eyes momentarily flared wide before he seemed to catch himself. "Accidents happen."

Violet shook her head, the pounding growing behind her eyes. "I should have been more careful. I know not to leave a burning candle unattended." She fisted her hand and pressed it to her forehead. "This is all my fault." She took a sip of coffee to both hide her tears and fight the nausea welling in the pit of her stomach.

Chad squeezed her free hand. "Everything will be okay." He looked as sick as she felt.

Violet knew she was to blame with the certainty of a person who knew her life had taken a long, windy detour without any street signs or road maps to guide her.

If Violet had felt lost after Abby's death, she felt absolutely adrift now.

"This is my fault." Her voice came out hoarse and soft. "My fault."

Just like Abby's murder had been her fault, too.

CHAPTER 14

he automatic doors of the hospital whirred open and a rush of warm heat whooshed across Violet's already flushed cheeks. She had tried to call Theo on his cell phone, but he wasn't picking up. Part of her wanted to believe he was following some rule about no cell phone use at the hospital, if those rules still existed. But the stark reality was like a knife twisting in her gut.

Theo probably had no desire to talk to her ever again.

Who left a child alone? And then the worst possible thing happened. Well, almost the worst.

Theo might not want to see her, but she *had* to see Liam for herself. Make sure he was okay. If not, she'd go out of her mind.

While driving to the hospital, Violet had prayed the entire way for Liam's well-being. Initially, Chad had offered to drive her to the hospital, but then he had to stay back to deal with the fire department. After answering a few questions of her own—why had she left a candle burning?—she had grown impatient and left without Chad. Surprisingly, as she repeated prayers over and over in her head while she drove, she had forgotten to do her mental body scan for potential panic symptoms.

Strange how things worked. The more she got outside herself, the less she manufactured panic symptoms.

Unbuttoning her sweater, Violet slowed by the receptionist's desk in the lobby of the small town hospital. It took her a moment to find her voice. "I'm here to check on a patient who just came in. Liam Cooper."

Please, please, Lord, let Liam be okay. She remembered news stories of children being pulled from pools who seemed okay, but then died at hospitals from secondary drowning. Did this thing happen to kids with smoke inhalation? Her stomach dropped at the thought.

Dear Lord, please let Liam be okay.

Behind the desk, the elderly woman dressed in a pink smock smiled, an expression that seemed more practiced than genuine. Her white name tag read Marge, punched out from one of those label makers Violet once used to label her shoe boxes when she thought it was a good idea to organize her closet. Marge turned toward the computer at her workstation and widened her eyes, as if surprised to see the large monitor in front of her. She lifted her readers on the chain around her neck to her eyes and tilted her head back to study the keyboard. Each precious key stroke seemed to take an eternity. Violet's forced smile felt fragile the longer she held it.

"Do you have identification? A driver's license?" The woman said, tilting her head even farther back to look at Violet through the lenses of her glasses.

Violet dug out her driver's license with shaky fingers and handed it to Marge. The little patience she had ebbed out of her.

The volunteer smiled and looked into Violet's eyes as if to say, *Don't I know you?*

Violet got that sometimes, being the daughter of Jacque Caldwell. But rarely around Hunters Ridge. People sometimes saw her in a photograph with her mother, but mostly she tried to stay anonymous. She had even kept the last name her mother had created for her when she moved to Hunters Ridge. It made Violet feel safe. Safer.

Marge handed the license back. "Let me see if I can find the information you need."

"Yes, Liam Cooper is in—" She lifted her shaky hand to the monitor and squinted and dragged it across the screen to line it up "—Room 115."

Hope swelled in Violet's chest. "He's already in a room? He's not in the ER?" That had to be a good sign, right?

The woman tore off a purple "visitor" sticker from a roll affixed to the underside of the counter and handed it to Violet, then pointed down to her right. "115 is down the west hall. Due to privacy laws, I can't tell you any information about the patient."

"I understand. Thank you." Violet's voice cracked on the simple expression of gratitude.

She turned and strode quickly down the hall, doing everything in her power not to break out into an all-out sprint. Her heart thundered in her ears.

Dear Lord, please let Liam be okay.

Her simple prayer had become a constant refrain in her heart. She found it comforting—and distracting.

Violet pushed open the door to the far wing of the hospital. She froze when she saw Theo talking to a nurse midway down the hall. He plowed a hand through his hair and leaned back...in grief? In relief? She couldn't decipher between the two very different emotions from this far away.

The hot surge of blood in her ears deafened her. The hallway stretched into a narrow tunnel with pulsating walls.

Fighting back the sensations crowding in on her, she took a step forward. Theo turned and saw her approaching.

His body stilled.

When she reached him, she bowed her head, unable to force the words past her lips. She drew in a deep breath and lifted her chin to meet his concerned gaze. "How is Liam?"

Theo touched her arm and gave her a quick nod. A ghost of a smile touched the corners of his mouth. Even before he said anything, relief washed over her. She flattened her palm on his solid chest; the need to ground herself was overwhelming.

"He's okay?" she whispered. "He's really okay?"

Theo nodded. "He's okay. The doctor wants to keep him under observation overnight. Liam had asthmatic symptoms when he was a baby, so she's keeping him out of an abundance of caution."

"Can I see him?" Tears blurred her vision. She had never been more grateful.

Thank you, Lord.

Theo nodded. "He's sleeping, but go on in."

Violet looked up at him and they locked gazes for a long minute. "Thank you," she whispered. She slipped past him and stopped at the end of Liam's bed. The last time she had seen the little guy was when he had fallen asleep while she was reading him stories. She bowed her head and felt the flood of tears coming.

"What is it?" Theo asked, his voice thick with concern.

"I'm sorry." The need to explain, to ease the guilt weighing on her chest, was strong. "He had fallen asleep on the couch and I slipped out to get him a snack from the break room." She shook her head, searching the recesses of her mind. "I couldn't have been gone that long…"

She lifted a shaky hand to her forehead.

"When I came back, I saw the smoke. Black smoke." She

sniffed. "I'm so, so sorry. I bring trouble wherever I go. It's dangerous to be around me."

First Abby, now this…

If only I hadn't lit the candle.

She had to admit her mistake to Theo. Clear her conscience.

"Dad…" Liam said in a groggy voice.

Violet and Theo both turned toward the bed.

"Sorry, did we wake you buddy?" Theo whispered.

"Where am I?" Liam mumbled.

"You're okay." Theo walked around to the other side of the bed and took his son's hand in his and brought it to his lips. "You gave us a little scare, is all."

"Is the trailer on fire?" Liam asked, his eyes wide, the deep brown color so much like his dad's.

Theo cut her a sideways glance before turning his attention back to his son. "The firefighters took care of it. Don't worry." He patted his son's hand. "Do you remember anything?"

Liam narrowed his gaze. "I couldn't open the door. I was all by myself."

Violet wrapped her hands around the bedside rail and squeezed. "I'm sorry. I went to get you hot chocolate and cookies."

Liam scrunched up his nose. "I fell asleep when you were reading me a book, but I woke up to a crashing sound. And then I smelled smoke and I couldn't open the door."

Violet and Theo exchanged confused gazes.

"You heard a crash?" Theo asked.

"Yeah." A faraway look descended in Liam's eyes as if he were remembering something. "It sounded like when I hit the ball and it smashed the back window. Everything got smoky." Liam's lower lip quivered and tears welled in his eyes. "I couldn't open the door. So I got down on the floor." His nostrils flared and Violet's heart broke.

She reached out and touched his leg. "I'm sorry I left you alone." What had he heard? Had the window exploded from the heat?

Theo ran his knuckles across his son's pale cheek. "All that matters is that you're safe now. You're safe now."

Violet pressed a kiss to Liam's forehead. "I need to talk to your daddy in private. We'll be right back, okay?"

He smiled. Such a trusting little boy.

Violet tipped her head toward the door and Theo followed her. When they got into the hall, she turned around and faced him, nerves tangling in her belly. "There's something I need to tell you."

"What?"

"I left a candle burning."

Theo narrowed his gaze, apparently not understanding.

"I'm so sorry." How many times would she have to apologize in her life?

He turned around and rubbed the back of his neck, then spun back around. "But Liam heard a crashing noise."

Violet bit her bottom lip. "You think something else started the fire?"

"I don't know, but I think you're missing something."

"What?"

Theo held up his finger. He slipped back into the room and returned a moment later. "Your coat."

Something about the way he said it made her stomach drop. She took it, studying his expression. "What is it?"

Theo reached into the coat pocket and pulled out the bottle of bills. "These fell out."

Time morphed into slow motion as she recalled all the events that had led them to this moment. She wrapped her fingers around the bottle and clutched it down by her side, wishing she could melt into the floor as she braced for the interrogation.

"Who's Zoe Michaels?"

"One of my mother's assistants."

They locked eyes for a long moment. "It's none of my business, but…" He glanced back into the room where his son lay. "If this is who you are—"

"Zoe thought it would be good for my anxiety. I—" She shook her head. She didn't owe him an explanation. She had been working hard to overcome her anxiety through grit and determination. How could he possibly understand?

Theo's shoulders sagged and he plowed a hand through his hair. "If that's the case, you should have your own prescription, not take pills from someone else. That's how Jenny started, with prescription drugs illegally obtained." Something flashed in the depths of his eyes. "Liam can't have any more chaos in his life."

A chill worked its way up her spine. She wanted to say she understood, but the words sat like a rock on her tongue.

∼

Violet showered and threw on sweats and wandered downstairs. She poured a glass of wine, stacked wood in the fireplace and lit the kindling. Once it finally caught, she plopped down. She swirled the glass of wine, staring through the burgundy liquid at the dancing flames.

She took another long sip of the wine, trying to let the tension from the day slip away.

"Rough day?"

Violet shifted on the couch to look over her shoulder. Betty stood in the doorway to the kitchen. "Yeah."

"Want to tell me about it?"

Violet put her wine glass on the coffee table in front of

her. She stood and got another glass of wine for Betty and handed it to her.

Her mother's housekeeper sat down next to her and shifted to face her. Violet poured out her heart to the woman who had been more like a mother to her than her own mother. She fought back the tears, fearing if she started she'd never stop.

Betty patted Violet's knee. "Liam's okay. Everything's going to be fine."

Violet ran a hand under her nose. "Theo's never going to talk to me again."

"He'll come around."

Violet swallowed hard. "If the fire wasn't bad enough, he found the medication in my coat pocket. I laid my coat down on the gravel for Liam when he was pulled from the fire."

Betty tipped her head, inviting her to continue. She had always been a wonderful listener, nonjudgmental and kind.

"Liam's mom has issues with drugs. He told me he doesn't want any more drama in Liam's life." Her voice trembled.

Betty studied her with kind eyes. "Do you have a problem?"

Violet slowly shook her head. "With drugs? No. I should have thrown the bottle out. They were a security blanket of sorts. I felt like as long as I had them near me, I could push through my fears."

Betty traced the rim of her wine glass with her finger. "If you need help getting through your anxiety, there's no shame in that. But go to a doctor. See what would work best for *you*. Don't take drugs like this—something from one of your mother's assistants."

Theo had suggested something similar. But that would mean admitting defeat. Acknowledging she couldn't battle through her anxiety on her own, without meds.

Violet got up and went to the front closet. She slipped the

bottle out of her coat pocket and stared at it for a minute. She handed it to Betty. "Can you take it to one of those medication drop-off sites? I'd do it myself, but—"

Betty accepted the bottle and slipped it into her pocket. "I'll take care of it." She pulled Violet into an embrace.

Betty smelled like home. "Thank you." The sound of her cell phone drew Violet's attention. "I should get it. What if it's news about Liam?"

"Go."

Violet untucked her legs and scrambled to reach her phone on the edge of the coffee table. Her heart plummeted when she saw her mother's number on the display. They hadn't spoken for at least three weeks. It was like she had some sort of ESP to call on one of her worst days.

"Hi, Mother." Violet forced a smile. Her mother could sense misfortune and she'd quiz Violet on how she might have brought it upon herself. She was uplifting like that.

"Violet! A girl should call her mother every so often. How are you?"

Violet sniffed and immediately realized her error.

"Is everything okay?" Jacque asked.

"I had a long day."

"A long day?" The grating tone of disbelief scraped across Violet's nerves. She could imagine a wine glass dangling from her mother's fingertips and a shoe swinging from her toes as she swayed her crossed leg. Violet's gaze drifted to her own wine glass on the coffee table.

Like mother, like daughter.

"I'm fine, Mother," Violet amended, not wanting to rehash her day to an unsympathetic listener.

"When are you coming back? We need you."

"It's nice to be needed."

Her mother laughed in a haughty tone. "You make it sound like you didn't already know that."

"I do. I just need more time."

Her mother sighed. "You've had a tough loss."

Violet held her breath, waiting for the "but."

"But…"

And there it was.

"…the world is a tough place. You were always too sensitive. You need to pull yourself together. Come back to work."

"Just a little more time. I'm helping out a friend in town with their record-keeping."

"Really? Who?" As if it were impossible for Violet to have established friendships in the years she had lived here.

"Theo Cooper."

"Theo? Why does that name sound familiar?"

"I'm not sure." *Because he was the boy who took me to the prom and broke my heart.* But her mother didn't remember silly little details like that.

There was that deep sigh again. "Don't take too long. I need you."

"Thanks, Mother. Good night."

"Night," her mother replied, an edge of hurt in her voice. She didn't like to be dismissed.

But tonight, Violet couldn't keep deflecting her mom's dismissive comments without destroying her soul.

CHAPTER 15

*T*heo had to squint into the black of night to see where the snowy road ended and the steep incline down the hill began. He hated how he and Violet had left things at the hospital earlier that afternoon. He hadn't been thinking clearly. The scare of almost losing Liam in the fire had made him irrational.

The sight of the pill bottle had also triggered something in him so deep, so primal, he lashed out. Jenny's drug use had hurt his son—their son—deeply. He had to protect his son.

Ironically, Jenny had come up to the hospital and kicked him out. *She* was going to protect her son. *She* was going to stay with him all night. Apparently, she was using this tragic event to be seen as the better parent.

Not wanting to upset Liam, Theo had slipped out, promising to come back in the morning.

Theo parked his truck in the circular driveway and climbed out. He hadn't called Violet ahead of time for fear she'd tell him not to come. He'd deserve that. But he played his hunch that she'd been brought up to be polite and couldn't ignore him if he showed up at her door.

Theo rang the doorbell. A minute later, Violet opened the door dressed in sweatpants and a purple hoodie. She stuffed her hands in her pockets and turned around and headed into the house. The open door was a silent invitation to come in.

Theo closed the door behind him. Violet led him to the couch in front of the fireplace. Two half-full wine glasses sat on the coffee table. "Can I get you something to drink?"

"No, thanks."

Violet sat down and patted the cushion next to her. "Is Liam okay?"

"Yes, his mom is staying with him overnight. Kicked me out."

"Hmm…" she muttered.

"Olivia called me about the fire."

Violet lifted an eyebrow, waiting for him to continue.

"The fire investigator determined that a Molotov cocktail had been thrown through the window of the trailer."

Violet dragged a hand through her hair and her shoulders relaxed a fraction. "That explains the crashing sound Liam heard."

"Probably." Theo nodded.

"It wasn't the candle."

"No, not a candle." Theo leaned forward, wanting to run a comforting hand down her arm, but he stopped short. "You're usually in the trailer at that time."

She looked up at him with wide eyes, coming to the same conclusion he already had.

"There's a strong possibility that whoever firebombed the trailer was targeting you."

Violet let out a long, shaky breath. "This is unbelievable. No one I care about is safe. What am I supposed to do?"

Theo rubbed her arm gently. "You don't have to be alone."

Violet bent at the middle and covered her face with her hands. Her shoulders trembled. "I can't apologize enough."

She shook her head. "I should have never brought my problems to your doorstep. I—"

Theo gently took Violet by both shoulders and pulled her toward him. "This is *not* your fault." He brushed his thumb across the soft fabric of her sleeve.

"I was naïve. I thought I could retreat to Hunters Ridge and I'd be safe. Like when I was a teenager. But..." She seemed hesitant. "What if the person who killed Abby followed me here? What am I supposed to do?" she repeated. "Go hide somewhere else? I don't have anywhere else to go." She probably had a million places to go, but he sensed she meant she had nowhere else she wanted to go.

The doorbell had them both snapping their attention toward the front of the house. Theo stood. "I'll get it."

When he opened the door he found his sister standing in uniform. She raised a skeptical eyebrow. "Why doesn't it surprise me that you're here?"

"Is everything okay with Liam?" His heart leaped into his throat.

"Of course." Olivia squeezed his forearm. "I would have called you if it had been an emergency. Don't look so worried. I'm here to talk to Violet. I'm assuming she's home."

"Yes, I am." Theo turned around to find Violet standing behind him. "Come in."

Olivia strode into the room, her shoulders square. His sister was a petite thing, but in uniform, she was a force to be reckoned with. "I just got back from the hospital." She held up her hand in reassurance. "Jenny's angrier than I've ever seen her. She wants me to press charges against Violet for leaving her son alone."

"Jenny has no right." Anger pulsed through his veins.

"I'm sure she'll settle down, but I wanted to give Violet a heads-up. I know Jenny has a jealous streak." Theo thought back to Jenny's overall demeanor when she rushed into Liam's hospital room. She seemed frantic, desperate.

Like a woman who'd almost lost her child.

He couldn't fault Jenny's anger. However, he hoped her gratitude that Liam was okay outweighed her unrealistic need to get revenge.

"Best if you give Jenny some time," Olivia continued.

"Okay." Violet's tone was reserved.

"That's only part of what I need to tell you."

Violet ran a hand down her hair, waiting for Olivia to continue.

"When I told Theo about the Molotov cocktail thrown into the trailer, he told me you had concerns about a stalker."

Violet's eyes widened. He had seen that look before.

Theo jumped in. "I didn't mean to betray your trust, but in light of everything else that's been going on…"

Violet crossed her arms tightly. "No one's ever been able to prove I have a stalker, but a string of events recently makes me believe someone's not happy I'm here."

"Any thoughts on who it might be?" Olivia asked.

"Before I came to Hunters Ridge, my friend Abby was murdered. Police in New York believe it was a robbery gone bad. I can't shake the feeling I was the target because she was killed in my apartment."

"I'm sorry." Olivia shifted her stance. "Any suspects?"

"No suspects. Yet, it seems crazy to think someone followed me here. Not a lot of people even know my mother owns this house in Hunters Ridge."

"We'll keep our eye out for any strangers in the area. I'll check with the motel, things like that." Olivia crossed her arms. "Anyone else seem to have a problem with you since you arrived back here?"

"Abby's brother, Elmer Graber, seems angry. Rightfully

so." It was obvious Violet still carried the burden of Abby's murder.

"Elmer was in the area right after the forklift accident I told you about," Theo added. "He used the lumberyard van to get home. Not unusual in and of itself, but the timing…"

Olivia made a note of it. "Amish kid." She made a face. "His name's not familiar to me, but I'll go talk to him."

"I—" Hesitation flashed across Violet's face. "I mean, the Graber family has been through so much." Theo could tell she didn't trust her instincts.

He touched her shoulder. "That can't be an excuse."

"I'll drive by their farm tonight. Get a sense of the kid." Olivia had a reassuring quality about her. "I'm capable of handling the Amish."

"Thank you," Violet said quietly.

"Anyone else likely to set your trailer on fire?" Olivia cut her gaze toward him. "Do you have any enemies, little brother?"

"I live a pretty boring life. The most drama in my life involves Jenny but she—" His blood whooshed through his veins. *No way.*

"Jenny's always been a hothead," Olivia said, her words doing nothing to quell the queasy sensation roiling in his gut.

Could Jenny have been that reckless? No, no, no. Olivia just never liked her. "She would have never risked hurting our son."

"Liam wasn't supposed to be in the trailer, remember?" Olivia said, tapping the bottom of her pen to her lip.

Violet gasped quietly and they locked gazes before hers scurried away.

"Listen, we don't know if Jenny did anything, but it's the sheriff's department's job to investigate it. I'll talk to the sheriff. He can send someone else over to talk to Jenny again. Someone with less history. I'll make sure no one talks to her in front of Liam."

"Make sure of it. Liam's been through enough."

Olivia nodded her assurance, then turned to Violet. "Anything else you want to tell me?"

"We've covered everything."

"Okay, I'll follow up with Elmer Graber and the department will follow up with Theo's lovely ex-girlfriend." Olivia smiled tightly. "We'll find out who's harassing you. Whoever set the trailer on fire could have killed you. Killed my nephew. I hate to suggest this, Violet, but have you considered leaving town?"

"She's not going anywhere." Theo put a possessive hand on Violet's back. She opened her mouth, probably to protest, and he shook his head slightly. She stilled. He turned back to his sister and kissed her on the cheek. "I'll make sure she's safe."

"Be careful, little brother."

Olivia, three years older, had been like a mother to him after their mother walked out. He knew she'd pursue this investigation with the same energy she expended trying to wrangle him when he was a wild teen.

"Now about you." Olivia looked at Violet. "Since you're apparently staying, do you have an alarm system out here? I imagine a big place like this has one."

"Yes," she said, her voice shaky.

"Make sure you set it. The caretakers live on the grounds?"

"Yes, Betty and Isaac live here. Their home is separate, but attached to the main property through the mudroom entrance."

"I'll stay tonight," Theo said, not realizing he was going to offer until he did. But what choice did he have? He couldn't leave her unprotected.

And he didn't want her to leave.

～

"I hope you'll be comfortable." Violet held a few clean towels to her chest as she led Theo to the guest bedroom which Betty always kept ready with fresh sheets.

Theo leaned on the doorframe and smiled his mischievous smile. "I think I'll be just fine. Thanks." He took the towels from her and their hands brushed in the exchange.

Sometimes Violet wondered how she had gotten here—how *they* had gotten here, and where exactly here was.

Tension buzzed around them and she took a step back and tucked a strand of hair behind her ear, suddenly feeling very shy. "Need anything else?"

"No." He held out the towels. "I have everything I need right here."

She glanced up to meet his gaze, then quickly turned away. Why did she suddenly feel seventeen again? "Goodnight, then. See you in the morning." She headed down the hallway toward her own room.

"Hey, wait up," he called.

She felt him approaching but for some weird reason, she was reluctant to turn around. Something about Theo shifted her world. Tilted it off its axis. Sometimes when she watched a romantic movie and thought about the "one who got away," she thought about him. It was silly, really. Juvenile.

The only thing they had in common was Hunters Ridge. And Hunters Ridge was only a stopover for Violet. A temporary respite from the stress in her life. But now the notion of a safe haven seemed ridiculous. She wasn't safe anywhere. Maybe Olivia was right. Maybe she should leave.

"Can we talk a minute?" he asked.

She turned around and furrowed her brow, trying to exude a curious yet nonchalant body language. Thankfully, he couldn't hear the thundering of her heart roaring in her ears.

Theo took her hand and led her into the guest bedroom. A loveseat sat in a corner under the window, a wonderful place to cozy up with a book and read. "Sit down."

She sat down next to him, feeling a little jumpy.

"I stopped over here tonight for two reasons. First to tell you about the cause of the fire and secondly to apologize."

"Apologize?" The movement of his thumb across the back of her hand distracted her.

"I was harsh with you in the hospital." Theo's face grew somber. "I had no right to go after you about the pills I found in your coat pocket." He bowed his head and cleared his throat. "But it set something off in me."

"I know. Jenny's history…"

Theo plowed his hand through his hair. "I got a phone call from Liam at work one Saturday morning shortly after I moved back home. He couldn't wake up his mom. I called an ambulance and we both arrived at the same time. Jenny was passed out on the floor." He scrubbed his free hand across his anguished face. "I don't want to think about what that did to him, finding his mom like that."

Violet touched the hollow of her neck, suddenly feeling self-conscious. "That's horrible. I'm sorry he had to deal with that. He's so young."

"I thank God everyday I was living back in Hunters Ridge so I could take custody of him. To be there for him."

"You're a great dad."

"So you can understand why I reacted so strongly when I found meds in your pocket that weren't even yours."

Heat flushed her cheeks. "But that's not how it is with me."

Even as her protest hung in the air, she realized how

common the words must sound to someone familiar with addiction. *Does anyone think "That's how it is with me"?*

The walls grew close and she realized she had to be honest with him. "After Abby was killed, I started having panic attacks." She let out a long breath. "Again."

One of his brows twitched. "I can't imagine what you went through. But why not go to a doctor? Why take drugs from one of your mom's assistants?"

"Panic attacks are a sign of weakness." Her mother's words. Jacque had zero patience for Violet's irrational fears, especially when they interfered with her lifestyle. She pushed thoughts of her mother aside. "I wanted to work through my anxiety without meds. I did it when I was a teenager. I had hoped that by coming back here, I could pull myself together again. In the meantime, my mom's assistant gave me some meds to get me through. I only took a pill once. I had them in my pocket as a security blanket. Anxiety is a major head game."

Theo rubbed a hand across the back of his neck. "I can't claim to know what you're going through, but I support you getting whatever help you need. I shouldn't have judged you. It was a knee-jerk reaction to my experience with Jenny."

Violet scratched her cheek. "No, considering your history, you had a right." She lifted a shoulder. "I was stupid."

"You were scared." Theo leaned forward and put a comforting hand on her knee. "I wish you could have confided in me. You are not weak. You are one of the strongest women I know."

Violet drew in a deep breath. She had always wished she was stronger, but kept her thoughts to herself. "Thanks."

Theo shifted on the sofa to look at her directly. He cupped her cheek in his hand, and tingles—good tingles—blanketed her skin. "I'm not sure where this is going, but we need to be honest with one another."

Violet swallowed hard but couldn't speak. He leaned in and brushed a kiss across her lips. Soft. Warm. Inviting. She blinked slowly. She had imagined this moment since he had first stepped outside his house in his tux the night of their prom. *He was so handsome.* She had insisted that the Weavers drop her off there, not wanting to remind him of the vastly different worlds from which they came. She wanted to be part of the gang for once. Not the girl who lived in the big house on the hill with the movie star mom.

She had wanted to be the kind of girl a nice boy could kiss goodnight. A promise of something more. A future.

Not the girl who would inevitably leave town on a whim. Hunters Ridge was never meant to be home. Not permanently.

Theo pulled away and searched her eyes, making her forget her swirling thoughts. He had a way of looking through her. No, looking into her heart.

His fingers moved into her hair and down the long strands. "You're good for Liam."

"He's a good kid," she whispered, all her nerve endings on fire.

"You're good for me."

Before she lost her nerve, she leaned toward him and kissed him, this time more deeply. He returned her passion and pushed her back against the sofa, the top half of his body covering hers. His hands explored down her sides, her waist, her hips, leaving a trail of awareness. Of need.

Of longing.

A little voice began to intrude. *What are you doing? You're leaving Hunters Ridge. Don't start something you can't finish.*

Suddenly Theo pushed himself to a seated position as if he had read her mind. He plowed his hand through his hair and groaned, then gave her a playful grin. Man, he was sexy.

Theo got to his feet and held out his hand and pulled her

up to join him. Her heart was beating out of her chest. He walked her to the door and kissed her on the forehead, the whole time Violet feeling like a giddy observer, wondering what was going to happen next. Wondering what she wanted to happen next.

Theo lifted her hand to his mouth and kissed her fingers. "This is where we say goodnight."

"Goodnight." The single word sounded shaky. Disappointment coursed through her heart, but her brain knew otherwise.

"Sleep tight." He traced his fingers down her sleeve.

Violet forced herself to move toward her bedroom on wobbly legs. She felt Theo's eyes on her until she closed the bedroom door behind her. She flopped on her bed and now it was her turn to groan.

"What am I doing?" she muttered to herself. *Theo Cooper...*

CHAPTER 16

The combined scents of woodsy sawdust and charred papers swirled around Violet's head as she plucked through what was left of the receipts that had been salvaged from the office trailer. A few days had passed since the fire, and the spark ignited between her and Theo. Neither of them had spoken of the latter, perhaps coming to the same conclusion: they had no future.

Her life was not in Hunters Ridge. Everything about his, was.

So, instead, Violet focused on her job in the newly relocated office in the back corner of the warehouse, within the break room. A talented Amish handyman had already erected temporary walls to provide some privacy.

She drummed her fingers on the desk, wondering how she should handle the loss of some of these records. She had already reached out to all of Cooper and Sons' suppliers, as well as their buyers. It would require some additional work, but it was necessary. She was definitely earning her keep. But the irony that the fire had probably been set because of her wasn't lost on her.

A dark shadow crossed her desk and she looked up. Chad stood in the doorway, leaning on the doorframe. "A little warmer in here?"

Violet smiled down at the winter coat she hadn't bothered to take off. "Not exactly. But I'm fine." Even though the fire in the trailer hadn't been her fault, she was done messing with space heaters and candles.

Chad pushed off the doorframe and ran his hand across its smooth wood. "The guys did a nice job, didn't they?"

"Yes, they did. Do you guys have plans on getting a new trailer or just moving the office here permanently?"

Chad frowned, as if giving it some thought. "We'll see how it goes." He scanned the room. "This might just work, though. Are you comfortable?"

"I'm fine."

Chad gestured toward her with his chin. "How's it going with the receipts?"

She lifted an order form and a flicker of ash floated to the desk. "I've been known to be resourceful."

"The same can be said of me. I scanned most of the buyer orders." He handed over a thumb drive. "I think you'll find all of my receipts here."

Violet raised her eyebrows. "Great. Thanks. This will be a big help." She accepted the drive. The quicker she got their finances in order, the quicker she could turn the files over to Theo or Chad.

What she'd do after that, she didn't know. Someone was still after her. Maybe she'd be safer in a new apartment with a doorman in New York. She rubbed her arms. She wasn't ready to leave Hunters Ridge. Not yet. Being around Betty and Theo made her feel calmer. But another part of her didn't want to put those she cared for in jeopardy.

Theo's stay in her guest room had been a one-night gig. He had Liam to look after. Betty and Isaac moved into the main house for the time being and everyone had strict instructions to lock the doors and keep the alarm set.

The only thing she knew for sure was that all had been quiet since the fire.

But too quiet made her nerves hum. She was waiting for the other shoe to drop.

"Glad to know we'll be in good standing," Chad said, snapping her out of her preoccupation.

"Of course." Violet held up the thumb drive and twisted her mouth, considering. "Between your records and all the suppliers and buyers I contacted, I should be able to piece things together."

Chad clapped his hand on the doorframe, then pointed his finger at her. "My cousin was right when he said you were the man—woman—for the job." He took a step backward. "I'll leave you to it. I have some business in Buffalo. Hope to be able to put our product into a few more of the big chain stores there."

"That's great. You and Theo have done an amazing job building up this business. Your uncle must be proud."

"Of course he is. He's enjoying his retirement in Florida." Chad crossed his arms and shuddered with exaggeration. "I think I need to go visit him. Get out of this cold."

Leaning forward, Violet rested her elbows on the desk and threaded her fingers. "Last year at this time I was doing business for my mom in Southern California." She stared unseeing. "Every day was sunny and no snow."

"Then why are you here?" Chad angled his head. "You must be a glutton for punishment."

Embarrassment heated her cheeks. She blurted out her standard answer. "Abby's death sent me reeling. Needed a little recovery time."

"Yeah, that had to be tough," Chad said. "Did they ever catch the guy?"

"Not yet." Violet couldn't help but wonder what Chad thought about all the recent events tied to her, but she didn't want to get into it.

Theo came up behind his cousin and patted his shoulder. "What's the big discussion about?"

Violet shook her head. "Nothing much. Just getting situated in the new office and filling in the holes from the receipts lost in the fire."

"Violet was just telling me why she was sticking around Hunters Ridge," Chad said.

"Oh." Theo lifted his eyebrows, waiting. "I thought she was here because we're not exactly organized."

"Hey, I make the sales. I do my part." Chad smiled and stepped out of the doorway and flicked his hand to say goodbye. "Let's hope that fire doesn't put us behind the eight ball."

Theo sat opposite the desk and paused a minute while Chad walked away. "My cousin's in a chatty mood."

"I'm more partial to the strong, silent type."

A twinkle lit his eyes. "Oh, yeah?"

"Yeah, so I can get some work done." She leaned back in the chair and tapped her fingers on the edge of her desk in expectation.

"Fair enough." His smile warmed her heart and she thought about how his lips had felt on her mouth, her throat…

She hoped he couldn't see the heat burning her cheeks.

"How's it going?" he asked.

She shuffled a few papers, happy to be on neutral ground. "I explained to Chad that I should be able to piece together the records." She fingered the thumb drive again. "Chad had backed up some of his records digitally."

"I didn't think he was that organized."

"Surprise!" she said in an exaggerated tone. "It'll take a little longer, but we'll make it work."

"Thank you." Their eyes locked and lingered for a moment too long, making Violet glance down at her hands. "How's Liam?" She missed him hanging out in the office after school this past week. He was still recovering at home after getting out of the hospital.

"He's good. Jenny and his aunt are with him now. He asked about you. He was worried you had been hurt in the fire."

Violet pressed her hand to her chest, touched by Liam's concern.

"Liam doesn't remember seeing you in the hospital. He must have been in shock." Theo apparently sensed her concern because he added, "Don't worry, I assured him you were fine."

Violet smiled and nodded. "That's good." She pushed a stack of receipts to the side. "Any new updates from the sheriff's department?" She found herself holding her breath waiting for the answer.

"No. A deputy talked to Elmer, but got more of the same. He's angry, but there's no evidence he's behind the attacks or the fire." He tilted his head to look into her eyes and answered the question she didn't dare ask. "And Jenny's anger has gone from a rolling boil to a slow simmer."

"Do you think she's that vengeful?"

"She's Liam's mom." That didn't really answer the question, but she didn't push it.

"I called the detective in charge of Abby's murder case. They still don't have any new leads."

"I'm here for you, okay?"

His words of comfort made her think of the other night on the sofa, and she didn't want to think about that right now. It made her feel too vulnerable and wish for things that could never be.

"Hey," Theo said, thankfully changing the subject. "Liam asked me to invite you to dinner tonight at the house."

"Oh, I-I..." Violet stammered, suddenly feeling like a bug being examined under a microscope.

"It would mean a lot to him."

"To Liam?" A warmth coiled around her heart when she noticed the smile lines around his eyes. Theo was such a handsome man. A kind man. The type of man she could see herself with if she could see herself settling down. And she couldn't. Certainly not in Hunters Ridge.

She studied the small space, the unfinished walls, the cement floor. This was not the type of environment she had envisioned herself working in when she was a young girl. She wanted to be like her mom. Travel the world. Be glamorous.

Make her mom proud.

She met his gaze and smiled. "You're right, I'd hate to disappoint him."

A slow smile curved the corners of his mouth on his handsome face. "I'll drive you over after work."

Violet shook her head. "I'll drive over in my mom's SUV. This way you won't have to go out at the end of the evening to drive me home."

"Are you sure? It doesn't feel right."

"I won't tell anyone."

He gave her a skeptical, lopsided smile.

Her heart kicked up a notch at the thought of getting behind the wheel, but she knew if she wanted to move forward, completely recover, she had to do things out of her comfort zone.

And tonight, driving wasn't the only thing out of her comfort zone.

~

Theo didn't feel like a gentleman by leaving Violet to drive over to his house for dinner on her own, but he knew better than to argue with her. Forcing herself to do things was a way for her to recover. He just wished the sheriff's department had some leads on who firebombed his office. Until then, he wouldn't feel comfortable leaving her alone.

When Theo arrived home, he placed the pizzas he had ordered on the counter. He looked around and found Liam watching TV with his cousin Noah. Jenny and her sister, Mandy, were out back having a smoke. He bit back his annoyance. They had arrived here early and let themselves in. He'd have preferred to meet them at the door and send them on their way after they dropped off Liam.

Liam's safe. That's all that counts, he reminded himself.

"Hey, guys," Theo called to the boys with a forced cheeriness he didn't feel, as he took off his jacket and tossed it on the back of a chair. Jenny sucked the joy out of his life.

Liam jumped up from the couch and raced over to his dad. "You picked up pizza. This means Miss Violet *is* coming?"

Theo crouched down to get on his son's level and gave him a huge bear hug. "She's on her way."

A swift breeze blew in from the back porch. Theo turned to see Jenny standing in the entryway of the glass sliders, a rush of smoke escaping her lips. "Who's on her way?"

Liam dipped his head shyly, but didn't answer.

"Miss Violet is coming over to see Liam. She hasn't seen him since the day of the fire."

"She's the reason there was a fire!"

Theo straightened and patted his son on the head. "Take Noah and run upstairs and find those books you wanted to show Violet. She'll be here soon."

He waited a few counts until the boys were upstairs and

out of earshot. Then he turned to Jenny. "Don't do this. Your son's fine. The fire was not Violet's fault."

"Don't treat me like I'm stupid. The sheriff's deputy came sniffing around my house." She narrowed her gaze at him. "You really think I'd do something like that? You think I'm that evil? We have a child together." She shook her head in disgust. "Someone has it in for her and it's not me."

Mandy slipped in from outside, apparently noticed the heated exchange and immediately followed the boys' laughter to the upstairs. Theo could hear her telling Noah to come get his boots on, that they were going home.

"Please don't discuss any of this in front of Liam. He needs to be a little boy."

"And he's not because of me, right? It's all my fault."

There was no talking to Jenny when she got like this. "Jenny, you can be a good mom. Just keep on the path."

She waved her hand in dismissal. "You think you're too good for me, but you're not." She narrowed her gaze at him. "You think you're going to live happily ever after with Violet, but it's not going to happen."

Theo gritted his teeth. He wasn't going to egg her on. He glanced toward the stairs to make sure Liam wasn't coming down. Perhaps Mandy was holding the boys upstairs, waiting for the argument to die down.

"Lower your voice," Theo said.

Jenny stepped closer and practically hissed at him. "She's going to leave, just like everyone else in your life. Me. Your dad. Your mom."

Bull's-eye.

"Stop, Jenny. Now."

"No, I'm doing you a favor because you're too stupid to see it. Violet's never going to stay with you. You're simply a convenient place to land when the big bad world has gotten too rough for her."

"Jenny," he warned her again, but she kept ranting.

"You think *I'm* messed up. You weren't in the bathroom the night of the prom. She freaked out. Literally freaked." There was a gleeful quality to her voice that scraped across his nerves. "She's crazy. It's easier to hide her kind of crazy behind designer clothes and an expensive haircut." She grabbed the door handle and twisted it. "Do yourself a favor. Dump her before she dumps you."

Jenny slipped outside, and as if on cue, Mandy came down the stairs followed by Liam and Noah.

Anger pulsed through Theo's veins, but he kept it in check for the benefit of his son. "Thank you for keeping Liam today. Looks like he's doing well enough to go back to school."

"Awww, Dad."

Theo tussled his son's hair. "I'll give you another day or two, if that's okay with your Aunt Mandy." Visits with Jenny still had to be supervised.

"Of course. Drop him off on the way to work tomorrow."

"I will. Thanks again."

Mandy patted his arm in understanding as she passed. "Everything will work out fine." Then she lowered her voice. "Jenny will chill. She always does."

Mandy and Noah slipped out the door. Liam ran over to the pizza on the island and lifted the lid. "Yum, it smells good." Theo watched his son for a minute. He didn't seem to be any worse for the wear. Maybe he hadn't heard him and Jenny arguing.

How many times did I pretend everything was okay in my house as a kid when my parents fought? He didn't want to be a problem, too, but his mom had left anyway.

"Hey, buddy, you know I'm not going anywhere, right? I'll always be here for you no matter what."

"Sure, Dad." Liam seemed indifferent as he hopped down

from the stool with a thud of feet on the hardwood floor. He opened the pantry and tugged on a package of paper plates until he freed it from between the shelf and the rarely-used crockpot.

Then he said a quick prayer that he and Jenny didn't ruin this awesome kid.

CHAPTER 17

*V*iolet slowed and turned on her directional, squinting to see the number on the mailbox at the end of the driveway. This was the address Theo had given her. She should have known by the magnificent play set in the backyard visible from the road. She imagined a kid could spend hours on it, even in the snow. Her excitement at seeing the play set shifted to dread when she saw Jenny reaching for the door handle of the car parked in the driveway.

"Oh, no." For a split second, Violet considered driving past the house to avoid a confrontation. Then inwardly she laughed. What happened to the woman who handled multi-million dollar business deals on a regular basis without backing down? Ever. She missed her fearless self. "Here goes nothing," she muttered and turned into the driveway.

She wiped her sweaty hand on her thigh, knowing she couldn't keep running from stressful situations. She had to face them head-on and learn to walk through her anxiety, no matter how uncomfortable it got. Besides, nothing bad would happen. Theo was close by. His truck was parked in the driveway.

Violet pulled up alongside the car and gathered the handles of the grocery bag sitting in the seat next to her. Politeness wouldn't allow her to show up for dinner empty-handed.

Violet waited a minute before opening the car door, hoping Jenny would get into the car and leave, solving the issue of making small talk. She made like she was checking something in the bag.

Out of the corner of her eye, she sensed Jenny hovering outside the window.

Feeling like a fish in a tank, Violet realized she couldn't sit in the car indefinitely. Taking a deep breath, she pushed open the door and Jenny moved swiftly toward her. Jenny's hip bumped Violet's door. A dull pain shot through Violet's leg where the door made contact.

What in the world?

"Oh, I'm sorry," Jenny said as she backed up and pressed her hand to her chest in mock apology.

Violet pushed the door all the way open and climbed out. They had gone to high school together, graduated together, but their lives had taken such different paths. Yet here they both stood in Theo Cooper's driveway, all these years later.

Oh, what twists and turns lives took. It was like Violet couldn't move beyond her past unless she looked it square in the eye.

"What are you doing here?" Jenny asked. Violet thought she heard a woman behind the wheel telling her to hurry up and get into the car. She must be Mandy, Jenny's older sister, and the little boy in the back seat must be Liam's cousin.

"Having dinner." Violet kept her answer short, baffled that Jenny would act this way in front of an audience. She thought she should explain to Jenny that her relationship with Theo was strictly professional. But a quiet voice told her if she tried to explain that to Jenny, it would come off as protesting too much. And really, was that the truth?

She dipped her head, afraid Jenny would read the truth in her eyes.

"How nice," Jenny said drolly. "Did Theo invite you?"

The dome light on the other car popped on as the driver climbed out. "Come on, Jenny. Let's go."

"One minute. We're talking here."

"Don't cause a scene. Liam's right inside," Mandy said.

"One minute," Jenny insisted, then turned back to Violet. "Are you and Theo dating?"

The car door closed, Jenny's sister obviously growing impatient.

Violet studied Jenny carefully, then said, "Liam invited me for dinner."

Liam's mother jerked her head back and Violet immediately realized her mistake. Violet should have said yes and not offered the whole truth. "My son invited you for dinner?" A deep line marred her forehead. Jenny had been a striking woman before drugs got their claws into her. Now, she was still pretty, but dark bags lined her eyes and her skin had aged. Violet hoped for Liam's sake that she maintained her sobriety.

Violet shifted the grocery bag to her other hand, then slipped her free hand into her pocket to warm her fingers. "He was worried about me." Jenny stared at her, slack-jawed, so Violet quickly added, "After the fire."

"That you're responsible for."

The venom in Jenny's tone sent icy dread pulsing through Violet's veins. She clamped her mouth shut, fighting the urge to defend herself.

"You had no business leaving Liam alone in the trailer that day."

"I'm grateful your son wasn't hurt more seriously." Violet wasn't looking to make any excuses.

Jenny's angry facade seemed to crack for a second before she braced herself again. "You might be used to getting what you want with your fancy clothes and money, but remember my son is flesh and blood. He's going to be destroyed when you leave him."

Violet's mouth grew dry. "I have no plans to hurt Liam."

"Are you planning to stay in Hunters Ridge?" Jenny shot her an accusatory glare.

"Hello, Violet," Theo called from the front porch. "Everything okay out there?"

"I'll be right in." Violet smiled tightly at Jenny, eager to make her escape.

"You're not going to move in on my family. This is *my* family," Jenny said under her breath so no one other than Violet could hear. "I've told you that."

"It's just dinner." Violet took a few steps toward the door.

"Cut your losses now. Save everyone a lot of trouble."

"Have a nice evening." The light reflecting on the windshield made it impossible to see Mandy behind the wheel. "I'm going in. It's too cold out here." Violet didn't breathe a sigh of relief until she was inside and Theo was helping her off with her coat.

"Everything okay?" Theo asked. He glanced into the other room to make sure Liam wasn't within earshot. "I'm sorry you had to deal with her."

"I guess as long as I'm in Hunters Ridge I'll have to get used to it." Jenny's caution about hurting Liam rang in her ears.

"No, you shouldn't have to deal with that. There's no excuse." He kept his voice low.

Violet heard footsteps pounding across the hardwood floor. Liam flung himself toward her and wrapped his arms around her waist. Feeling totally out of her element, she smoothed his hair, then crouched down and returned his embrace. Her gaze traveled to the window and she considered Jenny's warning that this was *her* family.

Pushing aside her feelings of uneasiness—Violet had been under so much stress lately, she wasn't thinking clearly—she straightened and tugged down the hem of her sweater. "Smells wonderful in here."

"We ordered pizza!"

Theo smiled apologetically. "I didn't have time to cook."

"That makes two of us. Well, technically, I don't really cook." She lifted her hand. "But I'm perfectly capable of picking up a prepackaged salad."

"My dad mostly cooks for the two of us because he says it's healthier than pizza and burgers from the takeout place."

"You guys do better than I do. When I'm traveling for work, I eat out all the time. I love to try new restaurants. Food from all different cultures."

"My dad says eating out is expensive. That we need to watch our money."

She pulled her sleeves down over her hands. In her eagerness to engage Liam, she had forgotten how ridiculously indulgent her lifestyle had been. She hadn't meant to appear that way.

Apparently sensing her unease, Theo said, "Liam and I would love to try different restaurants, but there's only so much variety at the Hunters Ridge Diner."

"I love their clam chowder and pies," Liam said.

Violet's eyes widened. "Oh, I haven't had one of their pies in a while. Maybe one day after school you and I can run there for a snack. If I remember correctly, I owe you a hot chocolate and cookies." A chill made her shudder as the memory of black smoke pumping out of the trailer came to mind.

"Can we, Dad?" Liam asked with his usual exuberance.

"Why don't we enjoy this meal first? Then we can plan our next one." Theo reached out and ran the back of his knuckles across his son's cheek.

Violet had a hard time reconciling this man, the warm, compassionate father, with the troublemaker of their youth. People did change. Find their place in the world.

Was that what she was doing, finding her way in this new world? Or was she biding her time, destined to break a little boy's heart—and her own?

Theo looked up and her cheeks heated when she found him studying her. He winked at her in his easygoing manner. "Hungry?"

The confrontation with Jenny had left her anxious, but now that she had time to relax, she realized that yes, she was hungry. Very hungry.

"Let me put the salad in a bowl," Violet said.

Theo smiled, then crouched down and pulled an over-sized bowl from a lower cabinet. "Here you go."

"Pepperoni pizza?" Liam flipped open the top box, ready to dig in.

"Let me give you a hand." Theo put a piece of pizza on his son's plate, then served some to Violet.

"Sit next to me, Miss Violet."

Violet glanced over her shoulder at Theo and smiled, then took her place next to Liam. She took a bite of the pizza. "Mmmm. Best pizza ever."

Liam pulled off a piece of pepperoni and dangled it above his mouth.

Theo sat across from them and offered first his son, then Violet, a napkin. An electricity charged the air between them.

Something about this domestic situation felt good.

No stress. No pretense. No pressure.

Violet dabbed at her mouth, keenly aware of Theo's eyes on her. "Thank you."

Half of Theo's mouth quirked up. "Any time."

A little part of her wondered if she had misread his silence after their brief romantic interlude the other night. Maybe it wasn't because he had changed his mind and wanted to keep things platonic.

Maybe it was because he wasn't the kind of man to kiss and tell.

$\sim$

Theo felt cozy with Liam's head resting on his shoulder. The little guy had fallen asleep on the couch.

Violet suddenly stood as if she had just remembered that she had to be somewhere else. "I should go."

Disappointment sliced through him. "Are you sure?" He gently put Liam's head on a couch pillow and covered him with a blanket. Theo stood and pulled back the curtain. A few inches of snow had accumulated in the driveway. "It is getting bad out there. I should drive you home."

She touched his arm. "No, no, I'll be fine. Besides, you'd have to wake Liam and he looks so peaceful."

"I know, but—"

"Please, I'll be fine."

Theo grabbed her coat from off the chair and held it out for her. She slipped her arms in and he smiled when her soft hair flowed over his hands. "Thanks for coming. Liam really appreciated it."

"Liam, huh?" Subtle lines of sadness creased her eyes, even as she joked.

"I did, too. You know that, right?" Theo dragged a cold finger across her cheek and hooked a strand of hair behind her ear. "I'm sorry you have to leave so soon." He leaned forward and brushed a chaste kiss across her lips. He feared starting something they couldn't finish.

She lifted a hand to her lips and touched them. "What are we doing here?"

"I thought that was obvious." A smile pulled at the corners of his mouth even as her question tossed a bucket of cold water over him.

"I know, but after the other night, we never talked about it. I had this whole conversation playing out in my head that you just wanted to keep things platonic."

"Gosh no. How did you get that?"

Pink blossomed in her cheeks. "We went right back to all business. I wanted to make sure you had an easy out. We both were emotional after the fire."

"You're good for me. You're good for Liam."

Her warm brown eyes drifted to where Liam slept on the couch. "He's a great kid."

"So it's not just me. You think we might have something here?" He studied her face. Something flashed in the depths of her eyes, something he couldn't quite read. Something he was afraid to ask about.

She lifted her gaze to meet his. "We both know I'm not staying in Hunters Ridge. As soon as I finish this job, I'm going back to work with my mom. It might be hard to believe, but despite all the crazy stuff going on, I've been feeling better every day. I guess when you face the worst, you get a lot of practice with handling anxiety. I'm not over it, but I'm dealing." She dipped her head shyly. "I finally scheduled an appointment with a physician. It's been a long time. There's no shame in getting help if the doctor feels it's in my best interest for long-term recovery." She shrugged. "Or maybe he'll suggest more therapy. But I'm done thinking I have to white knuckle it alone."

"That's great. You don't have to do any of this alone. We can figure this—*us*—out."

She pushed up on her tippy toes and kissed him on the jaw. It felt too much like goodbye. "You're a great guy, but you and Liam need stability in your life. You know that. I know that."

"So that's a no?" He laughed to hide the hurt.

"How would this be fair to Liam? He'd get attached and then I'd leave."

"What did Jenny say to you out front?"

"Her delivery was rough, but she had a point. A lot of people could get hurt if this doesn't work out."

"I'm willing to take that chance."

"What about Liam? He's had so much upheaval in his life already." Violet ran her hand down his forearm. "I don't want to hurt him. I don't want to hurt you."

Is she right?

Theo knew firsthand the pain of having his mom walk out on her family.

He took Violet's hand and squeezed it. "Let's not make any decisions right now."

Violet looked up at him sadly. "I don't plan on living in Hunters Ridge. I don't see how we could possibly have a future." Theo thought he noticed a hitch in her voice, but she squared her shoulders and opened the door and said goodnight without a backward glance.

Theo watched her climb into her SUV, turn on the wipers and roll down the windows to clear the layer of snow. She gave him a quick wave, then backed out of the driveway. As the taillights disappeared, he wondered what just happened.

$\mathcal{V}$iolet muttered to herself that she should have gotten on the road an hour earlier. With all this snow in November, it promised to be a long winter. A *really* long winter.

"I can do this," she whispered to herself in a cheery note of confidence she absolutely didn't feel. She was driving her mom's huge SUV. It could handle a little snow and so could she.

Deep breath.

Ignore the knot hardening in your stomach. Force out the crazy thoughts of crashing, passing out, losing control of the vehicle, and every other possible thing that could possibly go wrong. And most of all, forget about the disastrous note the evening ended on.

"You did the right thing," she spoke to the empty vehicle as a diversion. She had to cool things off with Theo.

Her cell phone rang and she glanced down at the fancy display on the dash. Hmm? Betty. She was probably wondering where she was.

"I'm on my way home," she said without saying hello.

"Pull right into the garage and close the door down behind you."

"Okay, I'm entering town now. Did you need anything at the grocery store?"

"No," Betty said emphatically, "come right home. The snow's really coming down."

"I just need some cream for my coffee in the morning. I'll be in and out."

"Violet…"

"I'm just running into the store. I'll park near the door."

"I'm waiting for you."

"Thank you. I'm going to go. Love you."

"I'd love you more if you'd listened to me."

"I'll be fine." Violet smiled. She loved that their relation-ship was more like mother/daughter than employer/employee.

Violet pulled into a space in front of the grocery store and ran in. She grabbed the half and half and was back in the car in less than five minutes.

She started the car and looked into the rear-view mirror and her heart stopped. An older model car had pulled up and blocked hers. Through the rear-view mirror, she studied the paint patches on its doors and side panels from where someone had probably tried to repair rust damage. Patience wearing thin, she tapped the horn. It was a polite tap even though she felt far from polite. A weight settled on her chest. "Move already," she muttered. The beginning of an all-out panic attack made her twitchy. Made her question her safety. Made her want to jam the SUV into reverse and ram the vehicle. Her SUV to his sedan. No competition. But what if she was overreacting? Surely she was overreacting. Some punk had probably stopped there for no reason, and now that she'd beeped he'd never move, out of principle.

Why park there when the rest of the parking lot is empty?

The slow march of panic that had started in her extremities had made its move up her arms to settle in her lungs. Her vision narrowed as her mind flicked through all her options.

She beeped again, watching the car in her backup camera.

A pounding at her window made her jump.

Elmer.

"Leave me alone."

"I need to talk to you."

Violet shook her head. "Leave me alone."

He pounded the window again. This time something loud clattered against the window, the sound slicing through her.

Violet scanned her surroundings, jammed the gear into drive, and pulled up over the empty storefront sidewalk to make her escape.

She pressed the accelerator to the floor and tore out onto the main road. Her heart pounded in her chest and made her queasy. She squinted against headlights reflecting in her rear-view and side mirrors. She couldn't make out the vehicle, but it was definitely advancing. Pinpricks of awareness tingled the back of her neck. Instinctively, she tugged on her seatbelt to make sure it was secure.

The vehicle grew closer. Violet slowed a fraction on the snow-slicked roads. Her stomach dropped. Definitely Elmer's old car. He rode her bumper now. She kept her speed consistent, praying the oversized SUV would stay on the road.

In the rear-view mirror, she watched his vehicle shoot out and make like he was going to pass her. She glanced over as he pulled up alongside her. He stared ahead at the road in front of him. She eased off the accelerator, praying that he'd just go on by. Maybe his anger hadn't turned to all-out recklessness.

As his tires spit snow and salt on the side of her vehicle, he finally turned to look at her, his expression blurred by the slush sluicing down her window. Holding on to the steering wheel in a death grip, she turned her attention back to the road. A curve fast approached.

Terror seized her lungs. She lifted her foot from the accelerator and Elmer's car shot past hers. Holding breath, she resisted the instinct to brake. Braking fast on snowy roads was a recipe for disaster.

Elmer swerved at the last minute. Ice and slush slammed into her windshield with a loud thud. She was amazed her windshield didn't shatter. Her wipers smeared the slushy mess, making it momentarily impossible to see.

Through the grace of God, she successfully navigated the curve, and the straightaway opened up in front of her.

"Where did he go?" she whispered on a shaky breath, glancing out all her windows and mirrors.

A flash of light swept across her rear-view mirror. She tapped on her brakes and pulled over. Trying to catch her breath and calm her rioting emotions, she shifted around in her seat to get a better view.

Elmer had smashed into a tree, and smoke poured from the front of the vehicle. Her raspy breath was the only sound. The stillness was more unsettling than the frantic moments before the crash.

With trembling hands, she slid her cell phone out of her purse and dialed 9-1-1.

"Yes, this is Violet Jackson. There's been a accident on Route 31 about two miles outside of town."

"Is anyone hurt?"

"I'm not…sure. A vehicle hit a tree."

"Okay, we'll send a patrol car and an ambulance. Can you see if there are any injuries?"

"I don't know."

"Can you check?"

"Um…"

"Only if it's safe. Don't jeopardize your own safety."

"Okay." Her mouth grew dry as indecision rioted within her.

"Please stay on the scene. We have help en route."

Violet ended the call. The blackness of the country road settled in around her and made her realize how truly isolated she was out here. She twisted around in her seat to get a better view but the rapidly falling snow had obscured her back window. She pressed the down control on her window and the motor hummed as it lowered.

The scene was eerily silent.

With a shaky hand, she pulled the lever and opened the door. Through the crack, she studied the crash scene.

The red taillights on the old car turned the snow a faint pink. A brisk wind hit her cheeks and slid through her open collar. She sensed no motion. It was doubtful Elmer would emerge from that mess and attack her. Suddenly a loud popping sound rent the night air. Orange flames shot out of the engine compartment.

"Oh no..." She closed her eyes briefly and whispered, "Dear Lord, please help me do the right thing."

With all her senses on heightened alert, she climbed out of her car, ready to retreat if Elmer appeared out of the wreck. Her stomach twisted as a little voice told her to jump back into the SUV and drive away. Let the sheriff's department and ambulance take care of him.

You owe him nothing.

The flames shot higher and the horrid smell of burning oil and rubber reached her nose on a gust of wind. Could she leave Elmer to die?

Holding her breath and her coat closed, she stared down the road, straining to listen for sirens, but she knew that even if they had been dispatched immediately, it would take a few more minutes until they arrived.

Adrenaline surged through her veins. She jogged toward the truck, her flat shoes slipping on the icy road, making her feel like a video of her might appear online under "World's Bravest" or, depending how this all unfolded, "World's Dumbest."

Violet's pulse whooshed in her ears as she got closer to the driver's side, half expecting Elmer to spring out from behind a tree and tackle her in the snow.

The heat from the fire made her cautious. As she approached the driver's side, she noticed Elmer's face had smashed into the steering wheel. Blood trickled down his forehead. There were no signs of an airbag deployment. The vehicle was too old for such safety features.

The fire would consume the vehicle—and Elmer—in moments.

She froze with indecision. Then she remembered Abby. The Graber family had been through so much already. Regardless of what he might have done, she couldn't stand by and watch him burn.

"Elmer! Elmer!"

No movement. No sign of life.

Dear Lord, help me do the right thing.

She plowed her frozen fingers through her mussed hair. Nerves tangled in her stomach as flames shot toward the passenger compartment.

Acting on instinct, Violet grabbed the handle and yelped, jumping back. The metal was hot. She stuffed a corner of her coat around the handle to protect her hand. The door didn't budge. She tried again, digging her heels into the snow for leverage and finally peeling it back. The hinges groaned in protest. The heat from the flames singed her face.

"Elmer!" Still no response.

Holding her breath against the acrid smell, she felt for a pulse. She was no doctor, but she did feel a trace of one, unless it was her own. The flames shot up higher. She sucked in a breath and coughed violently. The heat burned her cheeks.

Working quickly and without giving it much more thought, she reached across and undid his seatbelt. Bracing herself as best she could, she slid her arm around his back and lugged his heavy body toward the door. Unable to support his weight, she let him tumble out of the vehicle. If it had been any other day, under different circumstances, she would have thought it served him right. But out of compassion for another human being, Violet kept Elmer's head from hitting the ground.

Once he was on the ground, adrenaline gave her a strength she didn't know she had. She slid her hands under his armpits and dragged him away from his burning vehicle. She fell, exhausted, his weight pressing down on her legs as a loud pop and an explosion of flames shot out of the front end of the vehicle.

Just then, she heard a siren in the distance. She braced her feet against the ice-packed road and scrambled out from under the man who had tried to run her off the road.

Has Elmer been behind all the recent attacks?

As the patrol car rolled up and a sheriff's deputy got out, she suddenly started to shake, from fear. From the cold.

From doing something she never in a million years thought she could do.

~

Violet took a shower immediately upon getting home. Then she wandered downstairs and found Betty in the kitchen. The older woman wrapped a blanket around Violet's shoulders and rubbed her arms to warm her up.

"I told you to come straight home." Even though Betty

was admonishing Violet, there wasn't a hint of anger in her tone, only concern. And love.

The sheriff's department had allowed her to leave the scene of the accident and promised to contact her with an update regarding Elmer.

"He was so angry." A constant buzz of anxiety rippled through her. "I don't know how to make it better for him. I can't bring Abby back."

"You can't control how others feel or how they act." Betty bustled around the kitchen, putting on the kettle for tea. "He needs to remember his Amish upbringing and find forgiveness in his heart."

"At this point in his life, I don't think Elmer is worried about keeping the Amish rules. If he was, he wouldn't be driving a car. And trying to run me off the road," she quickly added. "So, I doubt finding forgiveness is high on his list."

The doorbell made Violet startle. Betty held up her hand. "I'll get it."

Violet followed Betty to the door. She found herself holding her breath until she saw Deputy Olivia Cooper and Theo. She almost cried with relief, but held herself back. It wasn't fair to Theo to hold him at arm's length one moment, then pull him close the next when it suited her.

"Come in," Betty said. "I'm making tea." She took charge and led the threesome into the kitchen.

Olivia opened her mouth to protest, but Violet said, "Come on in for tea. It's easier to just agree."

A small curve quirked the corners of Olivia's lips. Violet saw the resemblance to Theo in that expression and couldn't help but smile.

"Are you okay?" Theo whispered in her ear. "I should have never let you drive alone."

"You can't always be with me. And I'm fine. Really."

He searched her face as if looking for the truth. "I'm glad."

"Tea for everyone?" Betty added water to the kettle. "I could put on coffee."

"Tea is fine," Theo said and Olivia nodded.

Betty busied herself putting out teacups and a basket of tea bags while they all took stools around the large kitchen island.

"Where's Liam?" Violet asked.

"He's sleeping. My neighbor was kind enough to come over and sit in the house until I return." Theo brushed his hand down her arm. "I needed to see you."

The concern in his eyes touched her heart and threatened to make her break down in a blubbering mess. To save herself the embarrassment, she turned toward Olivia. "Is Elmer okay?"

"They took him to the ER. He had regained consciousness and I believe he'll be okay," Olivia said.

"Good," she muttered. She hated for the Graber family to suffer another loss.

"We do have news." Theo covered her hand. He cut a gaze to his sister, apparently encouraging her to go ahead and share the news.

"The sheriff's department found an accelerant, rags and bottles in Elmer's trunk consistent with those used in the trailer fire."

Violet leaned back on the stool, sighing. "Really?" As much as she wanted answers, she hated to think it was Elmer Graber, Abby's brother, who had nearly killed Liam.

Betty poured hot water into the teacups. "Can I get anything else before I leave you alone to talk?"

Violet slipped off the stool and gave Betty a big hug. "Thank you."

The older woman pulled back and gave her a confused look. "It's only tea."

"Thank you for everything. I don't know what I'd do without you."

Betty returned her embrace. "My pleasure, dear." She brushed a kiss across her cheek. "I'm going to bed." The Weavers were still sleeping in the main house so Violet wasn't alone. "If you need anything, knock on our bedroom door."

"Thanks." Violet pulled her hoodie sweatshirt tighter in around her. "Night."

Betty slipped out of the room. Violet turned to Theo, then let her gaze slide to Olivia. "What happens now?"

Olivia wrapped her hands around the teacup, but made no effort to dunk her tea bag. "Elmer remains in custody."

"Do you think he's the one behind all the attacks?" Violet was bombarded by a multitude of emotions.

"We still have to investigate. He hasn't admitted to anything, but after the evidence found in his trunk..." Theo squeezed Violet's hand.

"Did you talk to him?"

"He's very angry with you over the loss of his sister." Olivia tore the paper from the tea bag.

"Enough to kill me?" She had seen the hatred in Elmer's eyes firsthand, but it seemed at odds with who Abby was. Who the Amish were.

"Irrational people do irrational things." Olivia dunked her tea bag into the hot water.

"Elmer works at the cheese factory down the road from the lumberyard. He had every opportunity to harass you," Theo added.

"Nothing would bring Abby back. So why? What does he gain?"

"He was pretty wound up. He said you weren't going to introduce the devil to Lorianne. Let the outside world get to her, too."

Violet furrowed her brow. "I offered to teach Abby's sister how to do the books at the lumberyard." She held up her palm. "I hadn't had a chance to mention it to you, with the fire in the trailer and everything." She shook her head. "I can't believe it. Abby never got along with her brother. I don't think any of the girls did. He was domineering. Cruel sometimes. But this..." Violet hugged her sweatshirt tighter around her. "But the flat tire happened on the day I showed up at the lumberyard. I only met Lorianne that day."

"You had been to his house prior to then?" Olivia asked.

"Yes, I reached out to his family." She sniffed, hating how things had turned out.

"You became his target after what happened to Abby." Olivia set down her spoon. "In all likelihood, the attacks escalated as he feared you'd take Lorianne away from the family, too. But, at this point, it's all speculation. We'll cover all our bases before we close the investigation."

"Thanks."

"And Violet, you saved Elmer's life," Olivia said. "The fire would have killed him if you hadn't gotten him out of his vehicle when you did."

Violet tipped her head, emotion making her speechless.

"You did a good thing." Olivia touched her hand briefly. "Not everyone would do that." She took a long sip of her tea. "That's good stuff." She smiled. "Well...I'll go warm up the patrol car. I'll give you a few minutes to chat." Olivia slipped off the stool and her footsteps could be heard as she crossed the foyer and let herself out the front door.

Violet felt her cheeks flush. "I guess your sister thinks we need a few minutes to chat."

Theo stared intently into Violet's eyes. He lifted his hands and slid them into her hair. She sucked in a breath in anticipation as he leaned in and pressed a gentle kiss to her lips.

"I'm glad you're okay, Violet Jackson." He pulled her into a tight embrace. "It's finally over."

She pulled back to meet his gaze. "Is it? They haven't arrested anyone for Abby's murder yet. Elmer could be cruel, but he would have never killed his sister. And the likelihood that he went all the way to New York City…" She shook her head. "I don't believe that for a minute."

"You should call your contact in New York. See where they stand on the case. It's very likely they're unrelated. Abby's death was the reason Elmer had it in for you. That's all."

Theo gently brushed his knuckle across her cheek and dropped his hand. He kissed her forehead and took a step back.

"I know we're not doing this." He gestured from him to her with his hand. "But I'm relieved you're okay."

"Thank you," she whispered, unable to say more. If only their paths had crossed under different circumstances, just maybe…

CHAPTER 19

a few days later, Violet was in the new office, going through the receipts. Despite her efforts to recreate records destroyed in the fire by contacting suppliers and buyers, and getting help from Chad and Theo, something wasn't adding up. Something she probably would have noticed if she hadn't been so distracted by flat tires, falling boxes, fires and car crashes.

She rolled her shoulders and leaned back in the chair, feeling a headache threatening.

"Excuse me, Miss Violet."

She glanced up to see Abby's sister standing in the doorway, her hands clutched in front of her apron covering her Amish dress. Violet sat upright. "Lorianne." She said the name reverently, as if the young Amish woman might turn around and run away. Violet stood. "Please, come in. Have a seat."

Lorianne tipped her bonneted head. "I can't stay long." She fidgeted with the strings to her bonnet. "I wanted to thank you for pulling Elmer out of the car. I heard it was on fire."

So many responses swirled through Violet's head, but she settled on a simple, "Anyone would have done it."

"Well, thank you. I also need to tell you that I won't be able to learn how to keep the books like we talked about."

Violet reached back and lifted a stack of receipts. "Oh, you don't know what you're missing." She laughed awkwardly, but she knew there was a greater significance to Lorianne's job refusal.

Lorianne smiled tightly. "Out of respect for my family, I'm going to leave this job. I think I can sell some of my quilts for extra money. That's what my sister Ellen does."

Violet had often wondered why one twin had entered the workforce and the other one stayed on the farm. She threaded her fingers, hating that because of her, Lorianne had to quit. "I understand. But I'll only be here temporarily. Maybe your parents will allow you to come back then. After I've left."

Lorianne shrugged.

"How is your family?"

"We trust God will get us through."

"Your faith is admirable." Violet ran her finger along the edge of the desk, trying to muster the courage to say what she had to next. "I called the police in New York City."

"Oh?" Red crept up Lorianne's cheeks. Perhaps Lorianne's ability to forgive allowed her to move on without the answers Violet desperately needed.

"They arrested a guy in the neighborhood for breaking into a young woman's apartment. They have reason to believe he was targeting single women in the area."

"He was the one who hurt Abby?" The flat tone to the question was probably more painful than if she had fallen to the floor in racking sobs.

"They believe so. They're still investigating, but the detective seemed very encouraged." Violet allowed herself to be encouraged, too. Elmer had been arrested for harassing her in Hunters Ridge and a person of interest had been arrested for Abby's murder. Perhaps it was time to move on.

Lorianne smiled tightly. "Thank you for letting me know."

"You're welcome." It seemed like such a feeble thing to say. If Violet hadn't befriended Abby, she would probably be married to some nice Amish man by now and chasing children around the farm. "Please know that you're welcome to come back here. I'm sure Theo would say the same thing."

Theo appeared in the doorway. "What would I say?"

Lorianne tipped her head shyly. "I'm leaving my job here."

"And I assured her she's welcome back whenever she's ready."

"Of course," Theo said. "You'll be missed." A crease marred his brow and his gaze drifted from Lorianne to Violet, apparently sensing something was off.

"I need to go now. I hired a driver to take me home." Lorianne hustled out of the office.

Violet flopped down in the desk chair. "I wish she didn't have to quit."

"Yeah, it's not uncommon. Most of the Amish women end up running their homes. Raising children." Theo sat in the chair across from her desk.

A twinge of anger pinged her gut. "She's not even married yet. She's only leaving now because her family doesn't want her around me."

"Don't borrow trouble. Her family probably wants her close now with Elmer in jail."

"What a mess."

"Elmer created his own mess. You can't feel bad for him. He was reckless in his grief. He could have seriously hurt you." Theo's voice grew softer. "Or worse."

Violet wrung her hands and glanced down at the receipts in front of her. She needed to focus on the task at hand. "The trailer fire made this more of a challenge than I anticipated." Her annoyance at the Lorianne situation was evident in her tone. There was so much to be annoyed about of late. "I believe I contacted all the buyers and suppliers. Chad gave me a few receipts he had on file."

Theo leaned forward, resting his elbows on his thighs. "Chad or I can go through them. See if anything jumps out."

"That's what you hired me for. There are a few discrepancies I need to rectify. But I'll figure it out." She bit her lower lip.

"Having a party?" Chad joked as he stepped into the new office with a coffee in hand.

The new location of the office made it busier, with more distractions. It would be amazing if she could get anything done in a timely manner. She hated that she was in such a sour mood.

"More of the same," Violet deadpanned.

"I don't know how you do it. All that paperwork is tedious. Boring…" Chad dragged out the word, then lifted his hand to his cousin. "Yeah, I know. That's why you hired her."

"Maybe you can give her some help. See if she's missing any suppliers or customers. She has a few holes to plug."

"I gave you my files. Didn't they help?" Chad leaned over Violet's desk, angling his head to look at the computer screen. "I'm not sure why she has to go through all this effort. Couldn't we get some sort of waiver or something, considering the fire?"

Draping her arm over the receipts, Violet brushed her fingers across the touchpad on her laptop. "Don't worry, I'll figure it out. I've had far more challenging accounting issues when I was doing my internship for a big accounting firm before I got my CPA."

"Well, I guess we're in good hands, then." Chad lifted an eyebrow and turned to leave.

Theo caught Violet's eye for a moment, before she glanced down and typed away on the keyboard. She had to focus and wrap things up. She still wasn't back to her old self, but with each passing day she found a renewed urgency to get back to New York City, to get back to her life.

And away from Theo. It was too hard to work with someone she cared about, but knew she couldn't have.

~

Violet had gone through all the receipts and something still wasn't adding up. She had run through some credit card statements from shortly after Mr. Cooper's heart attack. There had been some large cash advances. Perhaps undocumented medical expenses? She had to talk to Theo about it.

When she arrived at Theo's house, Liam opened the door and smiled ear to ear. Violet's heart melted. She had missed him in her attempts to avoid spending any more time than necessary with Theo.

"Hi, Liam. How are you?" Violet asked, trying to relax her shoulders that were up around her ears to stave off the cold.

"Great. Did you come for my birthday?"

"Oh." Violet jerked back her head, startled. Somehow the fact that it was his birthday escaped her. Quickly recovering, she said, "Happy birthday."

"Who's there, Liam?" Theo called from inside the house.

"It's Miss Violet!"

Theo appeared behind his son, a surprised look on his face that surely matched hers.

Violet lifted her hands. "I didn't mean to intrude on Liam's birthday party."

"It's just me and my dad. I'm going to have a big birthday party with my class next week at the bounce party place."

Violet caught Theo's gaze. He nodded as if to answer the

unasked question, "Yes, I'm really that crazy to take a bunch of six-year-old boys to a bounce house."

Violet held up her hands. "I don't mean to intrude. I can talk to your dad at another time."

"No, don't be silly." Theo reached out and took Violet's hand. "Come in. We were just about to have fish sticks and corn."

"Oh." Her stomach did a little flip-flop. She wasn't sure if it was from the menu or his warm fingers on her cold skin.

Theo didn't let go of her hand until they were in the kitchen. He grabbed the mitt and opened the oven door. He pulled out a tray of fish sticks neatly in rows on a cookie sheet lined with foil. Corn bubbled away on the stove in a pot of water.

Liam picked up a stepstool. Holding it to his little chest, he carried it across the kitchen and put it down against the cabinets. He stepped up on it and retrieved a plate from the cabinet. He busied himself until he had set a place for her.

How could she refuse Liam's invitation now? It was his birthday, after all.

"Here, let me take that." Theo touched the collar of her coat and helped her off with it before she could refuse. He placed it over the back of a chair.

After Theo put the fish sticks on a serving platter and drained the water from the corn, they all sat down around the small table.

"This is my favorite meal," Liam said, happily dipping a fish stick in a blob of ketchup.

Violet picked up her fork, not sure if she should stab the fish that had somehow made it into the shape of a stick or if she should follow Liam's lead and pick it up with her fingers. "I've never had fish sticks."

"Really?" Liam asked in disbelief.

Theo snapped off the flip-top lid of the ketchup and

squeezed a blob onto his white plate. He reached over with the bottle turned upside down, offering to pour some ketchup on her plate. "So much better with ketchup."

Violet gave a slight nod of her head. She had eaten cuisine from all over the world, but she had never had this kid favorite in her own country.

She picked up a stick with her fork and swirled it in the ketchup, then took a bite.

"Good, right?" Liam asked, picking up another one with his fingers.

"Mmm…" Violet muttered noncommittally. She supposed anything was more palatable if it was deep fried and dipped in ketchup.

Theo watched her with an amused look on his face.

"Well," Violet said, not wanting to be pressed for her opinion on tonight's menu again, "I'm afraid I came over without a gift because I had no idea you could possibly be turning six years old already."

Liam sat up straighter in his chair and puffed out his chest. "I'm one of the oldest kids in my class."

Violet nodded, showing that she was impressed. "What did you wish for your birthday?"

Liam licked a smudge of ketchup from his upper lip. "From you?"

"Liam," Theo warned his son quietly. "You shouldn't—"

"Sure. From me." She smiled, enjoying how comfortable Liam had become around her.

"You said you used to go snowshoeing in the woods behind your house when you were a kid," Liam said, his eyes bright.

"You want to go snowshoeing?"

"Yeah. I want you to show me how so I can get good and then show my dad how to do it."

"Okay. Sure. We'll make plans to go snowshoeing, then."

"I don't have school tomorrow. Can we go tomorrow?" Apparently Liam knew it was necessary to pin adults down to a specific date and time, otherwise things didn't happen.

"You shouldn't put people on the spot," Theo said.

Violet set her fork down and smiled. "No, it's okay. It's his birthday and if he wants to go snowshoeing, then we'll go snowshoeing. And I think tomorrow would be perfect."

The phone on the wall rang and Theo pushed back his chair to answer it. He then held the receiver out for Liam. "It's for you. It's your mom."

Liam scooted off his chair and ran for the phone. Violet could hear him telling his mom that he was going snowshoeing, and Violet hoped that wouldn't cause more trouble for all the parties involved.

Theo leaned across the table. "You don't have to take him. He gets very excited and he can be very persuasive."

"No, it's fine..." Liam had suffered so much disappointment and loss in his life and she didn't want to add to that.

"Okay, if you're sure."

"I'm sure."

"I mean, you already took one for the team tonight. I can't believe you have never had fish sticks before."

Violet slowly shook her head, a warmth coiling around her heart at the genuineness of the man sitting across from her.

"Boy, we really did come from two different worlds." Theo squeezed her hand.

Violet raised an eyebrow, then picked up her fork and pushed the last fish stick on her plate around. "I never knew what I was missing."

"I'm sure." He dragged his thumb across the back of her hand, sending tingles of awareness across her skin. She wondered if he realized the effect that simple action had on her. "Was there something that brought you here?"

ALISON STONE

The hopefulness in his eyes made her decide a work discussion could wait. "We can talk tomorrow. Want to drop Liam off at ten at the base of the trail near the lake? I need to work up to the hill around the house. I'm a little rusty. I'll pick him up snowshoes."

"You don't have to."

"I want to," she said with a decisiveness that she hoped would put an end to the back and forth.

Theo smiled. "Sounds like a plan." Theo squeezed her hand again, then stood to clear the dishes.

As she looked around the cozy house, Violet realized that this was what she wanted.

Not a big, important job.

Not money.

Not world travel.

This.

Peace. Happiness. A family of her own.

But maybe Theo didn't want her. She came with too much baggage. Either way, she couldn't dare suggest a relationship until she was sure. She couldn't do that to Liam.

She couldn't do it to herself.

CHAPTER 20

The next morning, Violet pulled into the empty parking lot near the hiking trail and drew in a deep breath. As the snow fell, she felt a certain tranquility she hadn't felt in a long time. She doubted she would have ever dug out her old snowshoes if Liam hadn't asked.

Dressed in a snow jacket and snow pants, she opened the door of the SUV and climbed out. The bright sun warmed her cheeks, making the cold air bearable. Her pants made a whooshing noise as she moved around to the trunk. She had found her snowshoes in the basement of the big house and Isaac had dug up a pair of kids' snowshoes. She had given them the once-over and hoped the bindings would work with Liam's boots. She'd take him shopping for his own pair if he decided he liked the sport.

She tossed her snowshoes on the ground. She better get strapped up and give it a whirl before Liam got here so she didn't look so out of practice.

A crack sounded in the nearby tree line and a knot twisted in her stomach as she stared in that direction. *It's nothing.* She went back to getting ready. Over the past few weeks, she had to continually remind herself that she didn't have to be free from panic symptoms in order to live her life. That was all part of moving past her panic. *Feel the symptoms and act in spite of them.*

The knot eased a bit as she slid her boot into the bindings. She adjusted the straps, then attached the other boot. She lifted her foot with the snowshoe attached and smiled. She had been so busy working over the years, she had forgotten to do a lot of things, including taking time for herself.

She grabbed the ski poles and took large steps over to the deeper snow on a slight incline leading down to the lake. If Liam was up for it, they could take a hike along the path winding up the hill, or they could stay close to the parking lot and keep their hike on a level surface.

She dug a ski pole into the snow and kept moving forward, the sluice-sluice-sluice of her ski pants as her snowshoes bit into the snow giving her a sense of accomplishment.

The sweat pooled under her heavy coat even though the temperatures couldn't be more than twenty degrees, and she laughed at herself. She better get back into shape. She stopped and turned around. She'd have to wait for Liam before going any farther. The back hatch yawned open and she tried to ignore the edge of impatience intruding on the peaceful morning.

She returned to the SUV and took a sip of water. Another snap, like a tree branch cracking, drew her attention toward the shadowed path winding through the trees. The hairs on the back of her neck stood on edge. A reminder of the anxiety that always hovered just below the surface? Or her body's fight or flight response to a very real threat?

That was the frustration of having anxiety—the body couldn't always distinguish between the two.

Violet drew in a deep breath and let it out. *You're fine. Elmer's in jail. No one's going to hurt you.*

And Theo and Liam would be here any minute. She tugged back the sleeve of her jacket and saw that it was ten to ten. She suddenly wished she didn't have a propensity for being early.

That's when a shadow exploded from between the trees.

Terror seized her heart and a scream lodged in her throat.

Dressed in an oversized winter coat and a ski mask, the man yanked the ski pole from Violet's hand. Her snowshoes made it impossible to move quickly. He swung the pole hard and it connected with her knee. She let out a yelp and went down. The pain was excruciating as her knee bent at an awkward angle. Her boots snapped out of their bindings, leaving her sitting in the snow looking up at a masked man.

"Please, leave me alone," she whispered. "Please don't hurt me."

He lifted the pole and swung it hard. It landed across her right arm with a thwack. Her bulky winter jacket buffered some of the sting.

Tears blurred her vision as she lifted her hands. "Please, don't."

Something made the man freeze and they locked gazes. Something familiar around his eyes made her blood run cold. Did she dare let on that she recognized him? Would that make things better or worse?

How much worse could things get if he was going to pummel her with her own ski pole?

"You couldn't leave things alone." The man lifted the front of the ski mask.

Chad Cooper stared at her with an angry expression unlike any she had ever seen. A dark bruise colored his cheek.

"Stop, please. Don't hurt me."

"I'm not going to prison." Chad reached into his coat pocket and pulled out a gun.

Violet tried to stand up by pushing her gloved hands into the snow, but her knee was out of whack. She thought she'd have a better chance of reasoning with him if they were on the same level. Instead, she had to sit in the snow and look up at him and plead for her life.

What's going on?

"Why are you doing this, Chad?" Her voice sounded hollow in her ears.

Dear Lord, please help me.

A slow smile crept up his face. Violet hardly knew Chad —he seemed to make himself scarce around Cooper and Sons Lumber—but she had never imagined this. Why was he attacking her? "Whatever trouble you're in, you don't have to do this."

"You know darn well why I have to do this. You just won't stop…"

A band tightened around her chest. *Of course.* The financial records she couldn't reconcile.

He ran a shaky hand across his hair and puffed out a heavy breath on a cloud of vapors. "I never meant to," he said, rather cryptically.

"Whatever you did, we can fix it."

Chad looked off in the distance, a look of desperation on his face. "They're after me. I'm in too deep. I need some time to fix it and I can't do that with you in the way."

"And hurting me is going to help?" Her voice cracked on the word *hurting*, sensing deep in her bones that Chad Cooper's intentions were far more sinister than to simply hurt her. He was out of his mind.

Chad seemed to snap out of it a bit and shook his head. He dragged a hand across his face, shoving the ski mask farther back on his head. He retrained the gun on her.

"There's no way I can pay the money back. And I deserved that money. My father deserved that money. My father and Theo's father took over the business from Grandpa Cooper. But all the money is flowing to Uncle Mick. All our hard work is going to pay for his condo by the ocean. I can't..."

Violet's heart raced in her chest. She wished she could get to her feet. Get away. But her throbbing knee was the least of her concerns.

"I still owe too many people. They paid a visit to me last night. They're going to kill me if I don't come up with the money."

Violet held her breath, allowing him to continue.

"I should have never stepped foot in the casino..." Chad's voice shook this time. His words seemed to be spilling out in a trancelike state.

"Hurting me won't solve anything. It'll cause more problems for you." A chill skittered up her spine and it had nothing to do with the cold snow she was sitting in. "I can give you the money," she added, hope threading her voice. "My mother's rich."

Chad stopped and stared at her, as if considering it. "No, it's too late for that. You'll tell Theo."

"No, I won't," Violet said forcefully. "No one has to know."

"I've waited. I've tried to dissuade you. You couldn't put the books together with 'just good enough.' But I can't have you poking around in Cooper and Sons' finances anymore."

Keep him talking.

Realization rained over her. "You set the fire in the trailer. You almost killed your nephew." She tried to appeal to his humanity.

"I didn't see him..." Chad's voice trailed off and he grew more twitchy. "I did everything to try to stop you without hurting anyone. I flattened your tire, stalked your house, watched as you left the trailer..." He laughed, but his eyes

197

looked dead. "You should have been easier to scare away considering your history."

He knew about her panic attacks.

"What about the accident in the warehouse?" She struggled to keep her voice even.

"Hired a kid to keep track of you. Idiot took it upon himself to hop on the forklift and tip over some boxes." Chad ran the heel of his hand across his scrunched-up nose. "Total screw-up. If he had been caught, he would have ruined everything." He locked gazes with her and there was a hint of glee in his dark eyes. "I had you convinced you had a stalker."

"I don't understand. How did you know?" Her lower lip trembled as she searched past him, her eyes on the road. *Please hurry, Theo. Come on.* If Chad knew she was going to be here, didn't he know Theo was on the way?

"I overheard you telling Theo about your stalker back when we were all in high school." He tapped the side of his head with the gun. "I'm good at remembering that stuff. I underestimated you, though. I figured you'd run away if you thought he was back. Give me time to win big, pay back everything I owe." He let out a huff through his nose. "You don't scare so easy. But Elmer…" He laughed. "That Amish dude has some pent-up rage. Made it so easy to pin this on him. I hid the bomb supplies in his car and just waited for him to do something stupid. Didn't take long. He was bound to confront you. You were bound to call the sheriff. Figured they'd find the stuff in his trunk eventually. Him chasing you and crashing into a tree was just icing on the cake. What kind of sane person does that? Made it easier for people to think he had been harassing you all along."

"No one has been seriously hurt. You can turn this around now." Violet tried to push to her feet again and collapsed under her weak knee.

"Stop wearing yourself out. You won't get away." The certainty of his words made it difficult to breathe.

"I won't tell anyone."

Chad's dark gaze snapped back to hers. "Give me a break. You won't keep this secret. You'll go running to Theo."

Violet straightened, trying to act more self-assured. "I don't owe Theo anything. He humiliated me at prom by telling Jenny I was a pity date and she locked me in a bathroom stall. I made a fool of myself."

Chad's brow furrowed, as if he weren't following. "That was a long time ago. Who cares?"

"I care. Do you think people forget these things in a small town?"

An evil smile worked on the corners of his mouth. "I heard about how freaked you were that night." He jerked his chin toward her. "Why aren't you scared now?"

Violet swallowed hard, fighting the urge to run away screaming, if she hadn't had a bum knee. "Because I know you won't hurt me. We can work something out together. I'll give you the money."

The sound of her phone ringing drew Chad's attention. "Where's your phone?"

"My purse. In the trunk." Her words dragged across her dry throat. Tiny dots danced in her line of vision.

Chad held up the gun menacingly, and she knew even if she did try to run, she'd never get away with a hurt knee. Staring at her, he backed over to the trunk and reached in blindly for her purse, pulled out the phone and glanced at the display.

"Theo," he scoffed. "Must be trying to reach you to tell you he's going to be late. A big client asked for some new play set sketches to present to the executive board this afternoon. I called him myself. I told Theo it was a huge account."

Chad had planned everything, even delaying Theo and Liam.

"The sketches can't wait a single minute," Chad mocked. He tossed the phone back into the trunk. "Too bad you missed his call."

"Chad, please, I'm sure we can work something out."

He shook his head. "I tried to get you to leave it alone, and you wouldn't." He ran a hand across his nose and sniffed. "Shame whoever killed Abby didn't kill you instead. I hear it was a case of wrong place, wrong time."

"What are people going to think about me?" Her pulse roared in her ears. "Who will they pin my death on?" She swallowed hard.

"You coming back to Hunters Ridge has ruined my life, but I'm not going to let you screw with me anymore."

"You won't get away with this." Adrenaline surged through her veins.

"You think I don't have a plan? I'm not an idiot." His lips curled into a mirthless grin. "Elmer Graber was released this morning." Chad's affect was completely flat. "The Amish pooled their resources and posted his bail. Imagine that. I already had one of his friends call him. He hitched up his horse and wagon thirty minutes ago. He won't have an alibi. People will think he went crazy and beat you to death with a pole for killing his sister."

Dizziness overwhelmed Violet and she could no longer think straight.

"Get up. Walk toward the lake," Chad commanded, poking her with the pole.

Her gaze shifted toward the water. "I can't. My knee."

"Suit yourself." The angry look on Chad's face was the last thing she saw before his fist slammed into her face.

∾

Theo counted four rings before the call went to voicemail as his truck climbed the hill to the small lot next to the hiking path. He glanced over at Liam in the back seat. "She's not answering."

"Maybe she already went snowshoeing." His little voice carried so much disappointment. His default mode. Theo hated that.

"I'm sure she didn't hear the call. The path isn't far. I bet you we'll find her waiting there."

Theo glanced into the rear-view mirror and found Liam stretching against his seatbelt, searching out the window. He had decided the play set sketches for the new client could wait. His son couldn't.

Theo sighed with relief when he saw Violet's SUV parked in a spot by the lake. "Look, there's her car."

In his excitement, Liam unbuckled his seatbelt before Theo pulled in behind the SUV. "Remember what I told you about that."

Ignoring him, Liam scooted out of his seat and out the door. "Miss Violet? Miss Violet?"

Theo met his son around the front of the truck.

"Where is she, Dad?"

Instinctively, Theo scanned the area. The snow leading to the path through the trees had a single set of footsteps. He walked around to the front of the SUV and noticed tracks and drag marks leading to the lake. A single snowshoe had been discarded near the back tire. The other one was under the SUV. Something that resembled a broken ski pole lay in the snow about ten feet from the vehicle.

Theo's heart leapt in his throat. "Stay here, Liam. Get back in my truck and lock the doors."

"Why, Dad?"

"Just do what I say. Call your Aunt Olivia. Tell her there's a problem down by the lake. To come to the parking lot on the hill near the trail. To hurry." Without asking any more questions, Liam hopped back into the truck and Theo waited until he heard the locks click.

Maybe he was overreacting, but his intuition was screaming that something was off. Theo followed the path in the snow down to the lake. When he reached the clearing, he saw two dark forms struggling.

He broke into a full-out sprint and dove into the man dragging Violet.

Chad?

A rage like he'd never felt drove his fist into his cousin's jaw. "Get off her." He tossed his cousin aside and he landed with an oomph. Theo patted Chad's pockets and pulled out the gun and slid it in his own pocket.

Violet scrambled back, wincing apparently in pain. "He… he…was embezzling money from the company. He tried to cover it up."

Chad sputtered and pulled his legs under him to stand. Theo planted a boot on his shoulder and pushed him down. "Stay put." When Theo was convinced Chad wasn't going anywhere, he stretched out a hand to help Violet up. She stood and leaned heavily on him, favoring one leg. "You're hurt."

"I'll be fine."

Chad sat with his elbows resting on his knees and his hands hanging down between them, his shoulders heaving.

"You were gambling again, weren't you?" Theo asked, holding Violet close to him.

"I got in way over my head. People want their money back, and you had to go and hire her." He shook his head. "If she just went away, I wouldn't be here now."

Sirens sounded in the distance. Chad must have heard them too because his head snapped up. "You called the sheriff?" Fear flashed in his eyes.

"Did you think I was going to look the other way?" Disbelief and disappointment tangled in Theo's gut. His cousin had tried to kill Violet. "You set Elmer up, didn't you?" His cousin had been behind all the attacks. Had nearly killed his own nephew. Theo gritted his teeth, trying to contain his rage.

Chad sighed heavily, but didn't answer.

"If only you could have used all that energy for something good," Theo bit out.

Chad looked up at him with hatred in his eyes. "Everyone's not like you."

~

With the adrenaline ebbing out of Violet's system, the chill had settled in. Her head was throbbing and her knee hurt. But above all that, she was relieved as she watched Deputy Olivia Cooper lug Chad up the snowy hill in handcuffs. Theo practically carried Violet up, despite her protests that she was fine.

It was over. This time for real.

When they reached the top, Liam was chatting animatedly with one of the other sheriff's deputies.

"Miss Violet!" Liam turned and ran at her full speed. Theo held up his hand to slow his son down, but it didn't stop his fierce hug. "I'm glad you're okay." Theo's concerned gaze drifted to his cousin. That would be a tough turn of events to explain to the little boy.

"Me, too," Violet said, each word pinging off her aching skull. "I'm afraid we're going to have to reschedule our snowshoeing lesson."

"That's okay. I got to sit in a patrol car."

Violet couldn't help but smile.

"I'll take you home," Theo told her. "Someone from the sheriff's department can bring your vehicle home." Then he turned to Liam. "Hop in the truck, okay?" Liam did as he was told.

Theo turned to Violet and cupped her cheek. "You're the strongest woman I know. I'm sorry Chad hurt you. I'm sorry I didn't realize what was going on with the business. I should have been more vigilant."

"How could you have known? He was good at hiding it." She winced.

"Are you sure you're okay?"

"He hit me pretty hard in the head and my knee hurts."

"Forget taking you home. Let's get you to the ER."

Violet shook her head. "I just want to go home."

Olivia walked over, apparently overhearing the conversation. "Can we at least have the EMT look you over?"

"Sure." That much she'd agree to.

The EMT checked her out and told her what to do for the possible concussion and the knee injury, and to go to her doctor immediately if things changed. Violet signed some paperwork acknowledging she was refusing treatment against medical advice. She was not going to the ER. She wanted nothing more than to go home.

"Everything okay?" Olivia wandered over to the back of the ambulance.

"I'll be fine," Violet was getting tired of repeating herself.

Olivia touched her brother's arm. "I'll take Liam with me and drop him off at his aunt's house. The other deputy is taking Chad in." She gestured with her chin to Violet. "Get her home. Keep an eye on her, okay?" Olivia gave a subtle nod to the EMT.

"Thank you," Violet mouthed, afraid the sound would hurt her head.

They watched as Liam got out of his dad's truck and hopped into the back seat of his aunt's cruiser and waved.

For now, this all seemed like some awesome adventure for him. A story he'd be talking about to all his classmates.

Violet blinked against the bright sunlight reflecting off the snow. What had started off as a splendid morning now hurt her eyes. Theo guided her to his truck and reached around her to open the door. Then he trapped her face between his hands and kissed her, his lips gentle, warm and inviting.

"I don't know what I would have done if—"

She wrapped her hand around his wrist. "It didn't, because of you. Thank you." She leaned over and kissed his cheek. "Take me home."

EPILOGUE

ix weeks later...
Christmas Eve

Betty hung the last ornament on the ten-foot Christmas tree and stepped back. "Beautiful," she said with breathless awe.

Violet took a sip of wine and smiled. "It is."

When Violet came to Hunters Ridge this past fall, she never dreamed she'd still be here through the holidays. Well, if she had thought about it, it would have been because at one point she feared she'd never get over her anxiety.

But thankfully, she had been managing it quite well, thanks to getting the treatment she needed, surrounding herself with loved ones and faith, something she had forgotten until her return to Hunters Ridge.

"I haven't put up a big tree like this since you were in high school. Remember?"

"I do." Violet ran her smooth fingers over the soft needles. Betty's love for Christmas had offset Jacque's complete disregard for it. If anything, Violet's mother would breeze into

Hunters Ridge with a few gifts and right back out, as if staying here for any length of time would be too demanding. This year, Jacque was spending Christmas in Turks and Caicos. She claimed she was allergic to the cold. "In all the apartments I've had, I've never put up a tree. It never seemed worth it. I'd usually be on the road in some hotel during Christmas," Violet said.

Betty touched her arm. "I'm sorry your mother's not going to make it to Hunters Ridge for Christmas."

Violet covered Betty's hand with hers. "I'm happy to be here with you and Isaac. It'll be a wonderful Christmas."

Betty gave her a knowing smile, apparently appreciating Violet's attempts at making her feel like she was the reason Violet had stayed.

As if on cue, the doorbell chimed. "I believe we have a guest." Betty made toward the door and Violet stopped her.

"Let me." Excitement tangled in her belly at seeing Theo. She had seen him every day at work, but that didn't stop her from being thrilled now, too. They had untangled the financial mess that Chad had created, and his cousin had promised to make restitution to the company. Chad still wasn't out of legal trouble—his trial for all his crimes against Violet was scheduled for mid-January. But that was neither here nor there, for now. He wasn't able to make bail, so he wasn't going to be bothering anyone.

And the detective in New York had told her they were going ahead with charges against the man already in custody for Abby's murder. For the first time in a long time, she let herself believe it was over. She begrudgingly had to admit her mother was right in downplaying her concerns of a stalker. Perhaps Violet's tendency toward panic attacks made everyone seem threatening, even if they were harmless taga-longs who wanted to get close to a movie star and her family. All the same, she doubted she'd ever get used to that.

Violet smoothed a hand down her sweater and pulled open the door, determined to have one of the best Christmases ever. Liam burst through the door and peeled off his coat and boots and dropped them in a pile in the grand entryway. He caught sight of the tree and bolted toward it. Theo called after him to pick up his things.

"It's okay. It's Christmas. He's allowed to be a little excited. Let him go."

Violet hung Liam's coat over the banister and lined up his little boots on a small rug near the door.

Theo leaned over and pressed a kiss to her lips. "Hello."

She smiled and pressed into him. "Hello, yourself."

At that moment, Isaac, Betty's husband, came out of the kitchen dressed like Santa with a sack of gifts over his shoulder.

"Oh no, what is Santa doing here already?" Violet playfully put a hand over her mouth in feigned surprise. "It's only Christmas Eve."

"Santa has to get on the road. Ho, ho, ho. He thought he'd make a stop here first." Isaac rolled back and forth on the balls of his feet, getting into character.

Liam stood wide-eyed as Santa handed out gifts for everyone. Theo's son discovered he had a brand-new pair of snowshoes and a promise from Violet to finally take him out on the trails now that her knee was better.

When everyone finished opening their gifts and Santa left through the back door, Betty ushered Liam into the kitchen for hot chocolate. When Violet started to follow, Theo caught her hand gently and laced his fingers between hers. "I think there's a gift you missed."

Violet studied Theo for a long moment before he smiled, dipped his head and picked up a small gift tucked under the tree.

"It has your name on it."

With shaky hands, Violet took the small gift and unwrapped it. Underneath the fancy silver Christmas wrap she found a black box. Theo took it from her and got down on one knee.

Violet's heart raced. Her skin tingled. Excitement washed over her. All in a happy way. She pressed her palms together and touched her lips. "Oh, Theo..."

Theo snapped open the box and a sparkly diamond sat in a black felt holder. "Violet Jackson, will you marry me?"

Tears of joy sprang to her eyes. She pulled him to his feet and hugged him and tucked her face into his neck.

He pulled back and looked into her eyes. "Is that a yes?"

"Yes, yes, *yes*!"

He covered her mouth with his and they kissed for a long minute.

"Yuck!" They jumped apart to find Liam staring up at them. "Are you guys coming in for hot chocolate or what?"

Theo tousled his son's hair. "How do you feel about Miss Violet becoming your stepmom?"

"Pretty cool," Liam said. "It's about time."

Theo and Violet laughed, then Theo grew serious. He took Violet's hand and slipped on the ring. She held up her hand to examine it. It was a perfect fit.

The ring. Her new job. Her new life.

Violet Jackson had never been happier.

∼

Six months later...

"The newspapers are here. I put them on the stand inside the door," his doorman said cheerily. A little too cheerily for this early in the morning. The heat was already rolling off the

New York City pavement, emitting a sour smell of spoiled food, rotting garbage and festering humanity.

Altogether too many people encroaching on his private world.

He nodded without saying anything. People talked entirely too much. *Blah, blah, blah*...sharing all the details of their day without regard for who was listening or watching.

So careless...

He grabbed a newspaper and tucked it under his arm. The doorman probably thought he had been out for an early morning jog, but he had only now been returning from a night out in his black sweatpants and T-shirt.

But *he* didn't share his business. Never felt obligated to. That only led to more questions.

He jabbed the button on the elevator and waited, glad the doorman hadn't followed him. This particular doorman had a newborn son and liked to work the night shift because his wife—a petite woman with weary eyes—worked days at the makeup department at the flagship department store.

Entirely too much info. But people insisted on sharing, as if the mundane facts of their lives were pounding on the back of their lips, eager to make their escape into the world.

The doorman had been dozing when he slipped out late last night, otherwise he would have had to plan his return more carefully.

He shifted his train of thought, still in processing mode. Processing everything he had seen last night while standing in the shadows. It took him a good hour to come down from the high.

Blondie making her dinner over the stove.

The dark-haired woman so intent on reading her book on the fire escape that she never saw him one fire escape away taking photos on his smartphone. Don't get him started on that trend. People were entirely too obsessed with themselves. Always taking selfies. But at least that helped him blend in. Rarely did anyone question why he was taking a photo.

His nocturnal adventures also included tracking a woman past her prime making the walk of shame out of a nearby apartment building. He almost followed, but something made him stop.

Only the select few were worth more than a passing glance. Others intrigued him. Some, if they knew, would say he was obsessed. Maybe he was. But shouldn't they be flattered? Shouldn't they reciprocate his devotion?

The elevator dinged open and he stepped inside. He took himself and the newspaper into the studio apartment and locked the door. He crossed the room, the newspaper clippings tacked to the wall fluttering as he passed. He hardly read the headlines anymore, but it gave him comfort knowing they were there.

He poured himself some coffee from the automatic coffee maker. He had set the timer, as he had set his daily routine. He pulled down the shade on the window. Couldn't be too careful. Someone could be watching.

He drew in a deep breath. He loved the smell of coffee; it purged the smells of the big city from his nostrils.

He unfolded the paper and turned to the society page. It amazed him, the details people loved to share about their lives. Even though social media had been a boon to him, he still liked to cover all his bases.

There was something about being able to touch, see, *smell* the print of the newspaper.

He ran his hand over the bright smiles of an older couple —why did the rich geezers always marry younger blondes?— who were trying to stay relevant by giving an obscene amount of money to some obscure charity.

His eyes traveled down the page and his heart almost

stopped. Blinking rapidly, he couldn't believe what he was seeing. Were his eyes playing tricks on him after he'd stayed up all night?

He set his mug down and the coffee sloshed over the side, soiling the paper. He pushed back his chair, the legs scraping across the floor. He opened the kitchen drawer and removed the scissors.

Lining up the blades perfectly on the paper, he made a cut up the side, across the top, and down the other side of the article, careful not to slice any words.

He picked up the clipping and tacked it to the wall with the rest. He leaned back and read it again:

The daughter of movie star Jacque Caldwell engaged to business owner Theodore J. Cooper...

"Mrs. Caldwell's only daughter...graduated from...blah, blah, blah..." he muttered out loud, his excitement ramping up.

He couldn't believe his good fortune.

He continued to read out loud. "The ceremony will take place on August eighth in Ms. Caldwell's country home in Hunters Ridge, New York before taking an extended honeymoon..."

Hunters Ridge.

With his pulse whooshing in his ears, he ran to his laptop and flipped it open. He searched "Jacque Caldwell" and "Hunters Ridge." Then he did the same for "Violet Jackson." He couldn't find any real estate transactions in Hunters Ridge. His blood slowed to a sluggish *whoosh-whoosh-whoosh.* That's why he had never been able to find Violet during her teenage years, and then again when she disappeared more recently.

He traced Violet's familiar cheekbones in the photo. She always had been photogenic. Shame she hid from the spotlight. He had begun tracking her again when she got an apartment in New York City. Girl traveled too much for his tastes. Made it more difficult to watch.

But one night when she was back in New York, he got close. Very close.

Darn friend got in the way. How had he made that mistake? He had been so careful. So watchful.

A yellowing newspaper clipping on the wall about an unsolved murder made him proud. Below it was an article about an arrest in the case. He laughed. They were too stupid to realize they had the wrong guy.

No one will ever stop me.

He opened up a new tab on his computer. As much as he hated to leave the city where he stalked his prey, he decided it was time for a trip to Hunters Ridge. To finally catch the one who got away.

∼

Hunters Ridge Book 2
Learn more…
Go to AlisonStone.com

ABOUT THE AUTHOR

Alison Stone discovered her love of writing romantic suspense after leaving her corporate engineering job to raise her four children.

Constantly battling the siren call of social media, Alison blocks the Internet and hides her smartphone in order to write fast-paced books filled with suspense and romance

Married for almost twenty-five years, Alison lives in Western New York, where the summers are gorgeous and the winters are perfect for curling up with a book—or writing one.

~

Be the first to learn about new books, giveaways and deals in Alison's newsletter. Sign up online at AlisonStone.com

Connect with Alison Stone online:

www.AlisonStone.com
Alison@AlisonStone.com

Made in the USA
Middletown, DE
31 January 2021